"WHY DO YOU ALWAYS DO THAT?" SHEA ASKED WHEN she caught Teague staring at her for the second time in five minutes.

"I like the way you look when you're eating, as if every bite were an adventure."

She put her fork down. "But when you stare like that, I feel self-conscious. Like I have a milk mustache or something."

He stroked her upper lip with his forefinger.

She shivered in response.

"Nope," he said. "No full moon." He covered her hand, twining his fingers with hers. "I'm sorry if I make you feel uncomfortable, though."

Heat shot up her arm. She swiveled around to face him, intending to say, "Thanks for lunch. I'd better be going now." Only when she saw his eyes, smoky with desire, she swallowed the words and brought her free hand up to caress his cheek.

When he licked his tongue inside her mouth, a jolt of raw desire rocked her like a surge of electricity. *Lightning strikes*, she thought, dizzy with wanting him.

Kissing Teague was good, no doubt about it. Kissing Teague was very, very good, but kissing Teague wasn't enough. Not this time.

WHAT ARE *LOVESWEPT* ROMANCES?

They are stories of true romance and touching emotion. We believe those two very important ingredients are constants in our highly sensual and very believable stories in the LOVE-SWEPT line. Our goal is to give you, the reader, stories of consistently high quality that may sometimes make you laugh, sometimes make you cry, but are always fresh and creative and contain many delightful surprises within their pages.

Most romance fans read an enormous number of books. Those they truly love, they keep. Others may be traded with friends and soon forgotten. We hope that each LOVESWEPT romance will be a treasure—a "keeper." We will always try to publish

LOVE STORIES YOU'LL NEVER FORGET
BY AUTHORS YOU'LL ALWAYS REMEMBER

The Editors

AQUAMARINE

CATHERINE MULVANY

BANTAM BOOKS
NEW YORK · TORONTO · LONDON · SYDNEY · AUCKLAND

AQUAMARINE

A Bantam Book / June 1998

ISBN 0-553-44686-X

Published simultaneously in the United States and Canada

PRINTED IN THE UNITED STATES OF AMERICA

OPM   10 9 8 7 6 5 4 3 2 1

To Warren

Dear Reader,

Happy Fifteenth Anniversary, Loveswept! I'm proud and happy to be part of the celebration. To be part of the magic.

I remember when the first crop of Loveswepts hit the market fifteen years ago. I thought they were the best invention since sliced bread. Until that time I hadn't read much romance, but when my friend Doris loaned me my first Loveswept, I was hooked. Back then, though, I never dreamed I'd be writing Loveswepts someday. Who, me? Follow in the footsteps of Kay Hooper, Tami Hoag, Sandra Brown, Iris Johansen, Fayrene Preston, Helen Mittermeyer, and Janet Evanovich? No way.

Yes way. This month marks the release of my third Loveswept. So I guess the moral of the story is: Sometimes, if you wish hard enough, dreams really do come true. (Of course, working your tail off helps too.)

Loveswepts have always been different, special—category romances of substance. One avid romance reader from Ohio told me she reads Loveswepts because in addition to a terrific romance, they provide a memorable story. This month is no exception as Loveswept introduces a group of EXTRAORDINARY LOVERS, love stories with a little something extra. Extrasensory, that is. You know, "ghoulies and ghosties and long-leggety beasties/and things that go bump in the night."

I grew up reading Barbara Michaels, Naomi Hintze, and Marlys Millhiser, talented writers with a gift for combining paranormal elements with romantic suspense. So when the Loveswept editors first proposed the EXTRAORDINARY LOVERS theme month, I was excited, though as a new kid on the block, I never dreamed one of my stories would be chosen. But miracles do happen. (Or maybe it had something to do with my heretofore unsuspected telepathic powers. *Choose mine. Choose mine.*)

In *Aquamarine*, Teague Harris convinces Shea McKenzie to pose as his fiancée, missing heiress Kirsten Rainey. But when does the masquerade end? Shea soon finds herself falling in love with Teague. The problem is, she's not sure if Teague's in love with her or with Kirsten.

And she may not live long enough to find out. Someone on the Raineys' private island knows she isn't the real Kirsten because Kirsten isn't just missing. She's dead.

Or is she? An aquamarine crystal cluster may provide the answer and help these extraordinary lovers find their happy ending.

Catherine Mulvany

PROLOGUE

May 1998

Kirsten Rainey had been dead for almost seven years, dead and buried too, until an hour before, when Beelzebub dug her up. Luckily, despite his name, the black Lab was not in the least diabolical. He was, in fact, both sweet-tempered and intelligent, intelligent enough to understand and act upon the simple telepathic suggestions Kirsten planted in his brain. First *Dig* and then *Take me home.*

He crept up the stairs of the Raineys' summer home on Massacre Island one careful step at a time, a master spy of the canine persuasion. Three-quarters of the way to the top, he froze for a second or two in response to a muted howl of rage from the back of the house. Ruth Griffin, the housekeeper, must have discovered his muddy pawprints marring her immaculate kitchen floor.

Hide, Kirsten told him. *Hide before she comes after us with the broom.*

The Lab's ears went down, suggesting he was well acquainted with the business end of Ruth's broom. He tiptoed up the last few steps—or at least the dog version of tiptoeing—then padded stealthily toward Kirsten's room.

The door was open.

Silent as a shadow, Beelzebub slipped inside.

In the adjoining bathroom, someone was singing a slightly off-key version of "Bringing in the Sheaves" to the droning accompaniment of a vacuum cleaner.

Under the bed, Kirsten told the dog.

He dropped to his belly and wriggled beneath the bedskirt.

At last, she thought exultantly. After seven years of limbo, she was home.

The vacuum whined to a stop, but the singing continued, growing steadily louder until it too died away. "Holy moley! Look at that mud! Mama's gonna throw a fit. Beelzebub, you bad dog, are you hiding under Miss Kirsten's bed again?"

Mama? The singer must be the housekeeper's little girl, Glory, Kirsten realized. Not so little anymore, though. She'd be what? Fifteen? Sixteen?

"Turn my back for five minutes to suck up a few cobwebs and you sneak in." The eyelet dust ruffle was pushed aside and Glory's face peered in at Kirsten and Beelzebub. Not surprisingly, she didn't seem to recognize Kirsten in her present form. "Bub! What're you doing under there?"

The Labrador retriever cowered just beyond her reach.

"Come on out of there, you."

As Glory lunged forward, he sidled backward to slither out from under the bed on the far side.

"Doggone it, Bub!"

The Lab whipped around the end of the bed, toenails clicking like a family of woodpeckers on the hardwood floor. He lost his grip on Kirsten in the fracas, but she knew he'd escaped when she heard the *click-clack* of his retreat down the stairs.

"You better run, you worthless mutt. Better hope Mama doesn't catch you, either." Glory wound the vacuum cleaner cord and trundled the heavy machine toward the door.

She can't leave yet, Kirsten thought. I'm too vulnerable here on the floor. Suppressing a flicker of panic, she focused her mental energy. The crystal cluster vibrated, producing a low hum. *Look down.*

"What's that?" The girl spun around so fast that she tripped over her own feet and went down heavily on one knee. "Is someone there?"

Nobody but us ghosts. Not that Kirsten was a ghost in the traditional sense. She couldn't rattle chains or even appear as a chilly column of ectoplasm. She was, instead, a lost soul, the essence of her being transferred to the heart of the aquamarine crystal she'd clenched in her hand at the moment of death.

As Glory shoved herself to her feet, she noticed the crystal, half hidden by the bedskirt. "Hey, where'd this come from?" She nudged it with one finger. "Guess Bub must have dropped another treasure. Beats his usual decaying bird or half-eaten gopher."

Glory carried the stone to the window, where the late-afternoon sun sparkled off the crystal's many facets.

"Same color," she mused. "Same exact color as Miss Kirsten's eyes."

"Glory!" Ruth's voice echoed up the stairs. "Have you seen that wretched dog?"

Glory crossed her fingers. "No, Mama," she said. She set the crystal on the nightstand next to a framed photograph of Teague Harris.

Teague. Darling Teague. A flood of regret colored Kirsten's thoughts. Attuned to her mood, the crystal emitted a low hum. Sparks of light rippled along its surface like splinters of icy fire.

Glory, who was horsing the vacuum into the hall, paused on the threshold, whirling around as if she'd caught a flash of movement from the corner of her eye. "Beelzebub, did you sneak back in?" Then her gaze fell on the stone and she sucked air in a wheezy gasp.

The crystal glowed with an eerie incandescence, catching the sunlight and refracting it in a brilliant dazzle. It vibrated, reflecting Kirsten's sorrow for what could never be. The humming grew louder.

All the color leached from Glory's cheeks. Her mouth worked, but no sound emerged. With a whimper, she fled, shoving the vacuum ahead of her. The door slammed shut, and Kirsten heard the key turn in the lock.

Alone again, she thought. Though death had robbed Kirsten of touch, taste, and smell, it had honed her sixth sense to a keen edge. For some time now, she'd been aware of another, one whose very existence would throw the murderer off balance.

The final showdown was coming. She could feel it building like a thunderstorm on the horizon. At long last, the murderer was going to pay. Then maybe, finally, she'd be able to rest in peace.

ONE

Two months later

Teague Harris didn't believe in ghosts or reincarnation or any of that paranormal stuff. So when he saw his former fiancée—his disappeared-without-a-trace-and-presumed-dead former fiancée—sauntering toward him on the carnival midway, he thought he was hallucinating. Or drunk.

He *was* tired, no surprise since he'd been up almost twenty hours and had just finished a killer stint flipping burgers at the Kiwanis' booth, but damned if he was tired enough to imagine things.

He blinked. Twice. She was still there. Closer now. Which meant he could cross "hallucination" off the list.

And as for being drunk . . . okay, he'd admit to a slight buzz. Earlier in the evening, before the fireworks, he and his foreman, Nick Catterson, had split a six-pack to celebrate the new contract. And yeah, that was about three beers more than he was used to drinking these days, but hell, he was a long way from bombed, certainly not so polluted he couldn't trust his own eyes.

The woman was scarcely ten feet away and the resemblance to Kirsten was uncanny. Same long dark hair. Same triangular face. Same easy stride.

Just a few steps closer and he'd be able to make out the color of her eyes.

"Hey, Harris! Sounds like congratulations are in order. I hear you got the nod on the Massacre Island job."

Teague turned to face Joe Merchant, Crescent County's number one landscape architect and Teague's main competitor. He liked the older man, respected his ability, but they were still rivals. Normally, Teague would have gloated a little about his victory, but right then all he could concentrate on was the Kirsten look-alike. "Yeah, thanks," he said, and turned back to the midway. He had to see her eyes. Then he'd know for sure.

Or not.

The woman had vanished. He'd glanced away for what? Three seconds at the most? Yet she was gone. Nowhere in sight.

What the hell was going on? Maybe he *had* imagined her. Or maybe he was drunker than he thought.

Joe touched his elbow. "You okay, Teague? You look like you just saw a ghost."

Shea McKenzie strolled along the midway, nibbling cotton candy and thinking what an idiot she'd been to drive two thousand miles to visit this mountain resort town just because of an old postcard.

Two weeks earlier, shortly after her mother and stepfather had left on vacation, their home had been burglar-ized. While Shea was clearing away the mess the detectives had left behind, she'd found among the papers scattered near the open safe a color postcard of Liberty, Idaho. Addressed to her mother and inscribed with a brief, somewhat ambiguous message, the card had intrigued her, not just because her mother had evidently deemed it important enough to keep in the safe, but also because the picture itself fascinated her. The photograph of the scenic little town nestled beside a lake and surrounded by rugged mountains had triggered a strange feeling of déjà vu, strange since she'd never been west of Chicago in her life.

Shea had already been planning to drive to California to visit her godmother. Liberty was right on the way, she'd told herself. Why not spend the Fourth of July weekend enjoying the resort's amenities while keeping her eyes and ears open for a clue to the identity of the woman who'd written the postcard?

Enjoying, she thought. What a joke! Ever since she'd arrived in Liberty people had been giving her surreptitious sideways glances that made her wonder if she was walking around with lipstick on her teeth or toilet paper stuck to her heel.

As she debated whether to return to her motel room—carnivals were no fun anyway when you were on your own—her built-in pervert alert suddenly went wild. Someone was watching her. Again.

She paused on the fringe of a group in front of the shooting gallery and let her gaze drift casually over the crowd. He lurked in the shadows beyond the knife-thrower's tent, staring at her.

Being stared at didn't usually concern her much. Shea was no busty blond beauty queen, but she'd attracted her share of attention since hitting puberty. There was even, she'd discovered, a select group of males who actually preferred slim, athletic brunettes. So it wasn't staring, per se, that bothered her. It was the way this man was staring that had tripped her alarm. She felt threatened even though he was a good fifty feet away. His eyes seemed to drill right through her.

Suppressing a shiver, she told herself she was letting her imagination get the better of her. The man was probably just an off-duty carnival worker with time on his hands. After all, Liberty ran more to wildlife than nightlife. But whatever his motive, that expressionless stare of his bothered her.

Pretending a sudden fascination with distorted mirrors, Shea ditched what was left of her cotton candy and joined a family heading for the funhouse. She tracked the man in her peripheral vision and was somewhat reassured when he made no move to follow her inside.

However, her anxiety level rose a couple of notches when she emerged ten minutes later to find him still waiting outside, lounging with a loose-limbed grace against the trailer that housed the taco vendor.

Broad-shouldered and narrow-hipped, he was dressed in faded jeans and a loose white tank top that bared muscular brown arms. His dark hair was cropped short, and a hint of stubble shadowed his jaw. *Yeah.* Tall, dark, and dangerous just about summed him up. He was the type who inevitably turned out to be the hero in the movies, but in real life probably spent all his free time knocking over 7-Elevens, starting barroom brawls, and making lewd suggestions to women caught next to him at stoplights.

She wished she'd headed straight back to her room

after the fireworks instead of trying to prolong the evening. Single women traveling alone were targets for crazies, according to her mother. And maybe, for once, her mother was right.

Perhaps if she ignored him, he'd lose interest.

Then again perhaps he wouldn't. Even though she wasn't looking in his direction, she could feel the man's gaze boring into her. *Dammit, what is his problem?*

Shea angled herself so that she could keep an eye on him without being obvious about it. *All right, think, McKenzie!* But it was hard to think when every nerve ending in her body was playing hopscotch.

As she hesitated on the bottom step of the funhouse, the man straightened and started to walk across the midway toward her.

Adrenaline pumped through her veins. She dove for cover in a knot of lanky middle-schoolers.

"Hey!" protested a kid she elbowed as she worked her way toward the far edge of the tightly packed group.

"Watch it, lady!" said another whose toe she'd just stepped on.

"Sorry." She couldn't see her stalker from there, which meant he couldn't see her, either. She told herself that the thunder of blood pounding in her ears was the sound of opportunity knocking. *Now* was the time to make her move.

The kids migrated en masse toward the carousel, but she split off from the group, squeezing between the duck shoot and the ring toss next door. The dimly lit area behind the booths was deserted. She ran toward the far end, dodging hoses and electrical cables.

Breathing hard, she stopped behind the second-to-the-last booth to risk a quick glance over her shoulder.

No sign of Tall, Dark, and Dangerous. With her racing heart still drumming out a hard-rock version of "The William Tell Overture," Shea edged back between the two end booths and scanned the crowded midway in both directions. Where was he?

She spotted him at last, ten yards away with his back to her. Quickly, before he had a chance to turn around, she ducked into the nearest booth. Once inside, Shea heaved a sigh of relief. Out of sight, out of mind. She hoped.

Teague didn't even realize he was swearing until he noticed people around him giving him dirty looks and hauling their kids out of earshot. Hell, he'd lost her again. And this time he was pretty sure she'd given him the slip on purpose.

The question was, if Kirsten had come back, why was she avoiding him? It didn't make sense. Dammit, this *X-Files* stuff wasn't supposed to happen in real life, and sure as hell not in a sleepy little backwater like Liberty.

Located in the Bitterroots just west of the Montana border on the shores of Crescent Lake, Liberty's only claims to fame were a couple of played-out silver mines west of town and the fact that it had once—back in the heyday of the mining camps—been home to the state's most opulent brothel.

Only twice in recent memory had it merited mention in the Boise *Statesman*, once last spring when mud slides isolated the town for two weeks and once seven years earlier when millionaire Jack Rainey's daughter, Kirsten, was kidnapped from her father's Massacre Island estate.

The kidnappers had never been caught. Every once in

a while some clever local reporter would drag the story to light, pushing his or her own theory of what'd happened. But the truth was, nobody knew. Not the FBI. Not the dozens of private investigators Jack Rainey had employed over the years. Nobody. Both Kirsten and her kidnappers had disappeared into thin air. Vanished.

Just the way her look-alike had already done twice this evening.

"You wish your fortune told?"

Shea jumped in surprise at the voice close behind her. She turned to find a Gypsy draped in flowing scarves and glittering bangles, her black eyes sparkling with intelligence in a wrinkled brown face.

Shea shrugged, ignoring a little ripple of unease. Why not? Having her fortune told gave her an excuse to linger awhile longer. "Sure. I guess." She paid the woman and took a seat.

"I am Madame Magda. Do you seek to know the future, or is it the secrets of the past that trouble your heart?" The woman pursed her lips over ill-fitting dentures. Her bony, beringed fingers fidgeted with the fringe on her shawl.

"A little of both?" All she really wanted to know was why Tall, Dark, and Dangerous was so interested in her.

The Gypsy peered into her crystal ball for a full minute, then pushed it away with a grunt of dissatisfaction. "All I see are shadows. I need your hand. Your left hand." She rapped out the order.

Shadows? Great. Reluctantly, Shea extended her fingers.

She expected the woman to read the lines on her

palm. Instead, the Gypsy trapped Shea's hand between her own moist palms, closed her eyes, and began to rock back and forth in her chair. The wood creaked in a hypnotic rhythm. The lights dimmed. The air crackled with static electricity.

The old woman put on a good show. Almost too good. Where was that cold air coming from? Goose bumps raised along Shea's arms. Why had she agreed to this?

Suddenly the Gypsy's eyes opened wide, so wide a rim of yellowed white showed all around the irises. "Two." Her voice echoed hollowly, flooding the tent with sound and filling Shea's head with a deep, sonorous vibration. "Two from one. Two who are one. You." The Gypsy drew a hissing breath, squeezing Shea's hand with surprising strength. "Blood links you to the other side. To the other one. The secret's in the stone."

Then she released Shea's hand, moaned softly, and slumped back in her chair like a bag of old clothes.

Shea drew a shaky breath. "Madame Magda? Are you all right?" Tentatively, half afraid the Gypsy had suffered a stroke or a fit of some kind, she prodded the old woman's shoulder.

The Gypsy's eyes flew open, her pupils fierce pinpoints concentrated on Shea's face. "You must be careful," she warned.

Fear trickled down Shea's spine. She'd been to fortune-tellers before, but never one who was quite so convincing.

The old woman struggled to her feet to indicate that the reading was over. "Be careful," she repeated.

❖━━━━━❖

Teague Harris, you are one sick puppy. She had to be a figment of his imagination. But he started another circuit of the carnival grounds anyway—his third in the last twenty minutes.

Tired and thirsty, he stopped at a food stall to buy a drink. When he turned back toward the midway, stuffing the change in his pocket, he caught a glimpse of Kirsten's double as she emerged from the makeshift alley next to the Ferris wheel.

So he hadn't imagined her.

She flipped the hair off her face, a familiar gesture Teague recognized with a twist of pain. Not a double then. Impossible as it seemed, it was Kirsten herself.

A confusing mix of emotions—relief and joy, then confusion and anger—churned his gut. What the hell had happened seven years ago? Had Kirsten been kidnapped? Or had the kidnapping been a setup she was in on all along? If not, then how had she escaped and why hadn't she returned before now?

Her return made no more sense than her disappearance had unless . . . Had she heard the rumors? Was she worried about her father?

But, dammit, if she'd decided to return, then why did she run every time she saw him?

Teague shadowed Kirsten at a careful distance this time. No use spooking her prematurely.

Shea strode quickly through the crowd, trying to ignore the creepy-crawly sensation at the back of her neck. He was there somewhere. She couldn't see him, but she was sure of it.

The carnival swarmed with noisy life. Kids, up past

their bedtime, squealed with laughter. Music blared. Hucksters enjoined passersby to "Take a chance! Take a chance! Fifty cents! One half-dollar!" Teenage girls screamed with every swoop of the Zipper. Adults yelled good-naturedly at each other, trying to be heard over the din.

On all sides the colorful tide of humanity flowed around her in a warm flood. Yet Shea had never felt so alone, so vulnerable in her life.

She was nearly at the edge of the carnival grounds. Beyond lay the shadowy path through the park that was the shortest route back to the lodge, where she was registered. *Run*, screamed a cowardly little voice inside her head.

The crowd was sparse at this end, and she felt conspicuous in her red T-shirt. The safe haven of her room beckoned, but setting off down that lonely path through the trees might prove a fatal mistake if the stalker was still hot on her heels.

Shea paused at the exit to see if she could pinpoint his whereabouts. Unfortunately, the heavyset teenager behind her didn't anticipate the sudden stop. He plowed into Shea and sent her sprawling in the dirt.

"Sorry." The boy's apology was a nearly inaudible mumble.

She tested her moving parts, checking for damage, and decided she was only bruised, not broken. Her white pants were a dead loss, though, and, dammit, they were brand new. She sighed. "It wasn't your fault."

"Let me help you."

Shea grabbed his proffered hand, not realizing until it was too late that the hand didn't belong to the teenage tank who'd run her down. This hand wasn't pudgy and freckled. It was broad and callused and attached to a sinewy brown forearm. Her gaze moved up past bulging biceps to broad shoulder, muscled chest, white tank top. Her heart fluttered like a bird tangled in a net, and all she could think of was, thank goodness she hadn't set off alone on that dark, deserted path under the pines. As long as there were other people in sight, she still had a chance.

The small, discreet logo on his shirt said HARRIS LANDSCAPING, LIBERTY, IDAHO. Obviously, he was a local. Local what, was the question. Local pervert? Local rapist? Local psycho?

He pulled her to her feet in one smooth movement but didn't release her hand.

Shea tried to tug her fingers free, but the man had a grip like a vise. Her heart rate accelerated. She glanced up to meet his gaze.

A mistake. His expression was implacable, his eyes as hard and gray as the granite of the surrounding mountains. The corners of his mouth were twisted in a sardonic travesty of a smile. "I've been waiting for you, Kirsten."

Her throat went dry. Small hairs prickled along her forearms and the back of her neck. *Kirsten?* That was one of the names on the postcard that had sparked her interest in visiting Liberty:

> *Our Kirsten continues to thrive. If ever you need anything—anything at all—don't hesitate to contact us. Love, Elizabeth.*

Shea took a deep, calming breath. "You're making a mistake. I'm not Kirsten." Again she tried, unsuccessfully, to pry his fingers from her hand. The man was second cousin to a pit bull. "My name's McKenzie. Shea McKenzie."

"Prove it."

She lifted her chin. "Why should I?"

"Because if you don't, I'm going to haul your pretty little hind end down to the sheriff's office and let you do your explaining to him." His eyes glittered a warning. He meant what he said.

Shea's mind raced. Obviously, this was a case of mistaken identity. So the quickest way to get him off her back was to prove who she was. Or who she wasn't. "You don't believe me? Fine. Let go of my hand for five seconds and I'll dig my wallet out of my purse."

He eyed her warily. "If you're planning to pull another disappearing act . . ."

"No tricks," she promised.

He released her hand and she retrieved her wallet, flipping it open to display her Ohio driver's license. "See? Shea McKenzie. Says so right there in black and white."

He frowned. "ID can be faked."

"It's not fake. It's who I am. Ask my parents if you don't believe me."

"All right. How do I contact them?"

Shea cleared her throat. "Well, actually, I suppose you can't. At least not right now. They're touring Europe this summer."

He smirked. "How convenient. What about grandparents? Brothers or sisters?"

"Dead. The grandparents, I mean. And I'm an only child. But I have dozens of friends back in Ohio who will vouch for me."

"I'm sure they will." He circled her wrist with one hand and drew her a step closer. "You told them your name was Shea McKenzie and they have no reason to doubt it. Whereas both of us know different, don't we, Kirsten?"

She really had the innocent-bystander act down pat. Teague studied her face. Kirsten's mouth. Kirsten's nose. Kirsten's finely arched brows. And most damning of all, Kirsten's distinctive aquamarine eyes. Rainey eyes.

Despite her protests, this woman had to be Kirsten. And if her face weren't enough to convince him, there was the stubborn tilt of her chin, the athletic grace of her stride. Even her voice was Kirsten's.

He shook his head slowly from side to side. "Nice try, but I'm not buying it. How could I forget this face?" He outlined the contour of her cheek with his forefinger.

She jerked away from his touch. "Don't," she said. The pulse at her wrist raced beneath his fingers.

"Don't what?" He trailed the back of his hand down her throat. "This?"

She squeezed her eyes shut and drew a long, shuddering breath. "Just don't. Please don't. I'm not your friend Kirsten." There was a note of desperation in her voice, panic evident in the taut lines of her face. "You've got to believe me!"

A sudden doubt assailed him. What if he was wrong? What if she was exactly who she said she was? Lots of people had doubles. Look at all those celebrity look-alikes. "Oh, hell." He released her wrist and folded his arms across his chest. "Okay. Convince me. Prove you're Shea McKenzie, and I won't bother you anymore."

Irritation erased the fear shadowing her eyes. "You already saw my driver's license. What else can I show you?"

"A birth certificate might do it."

"Oh, sure. I always carry a copy of my birth certificate around with me." She fell silent, frowning in concentration. Then she gave a sharp exclamation. "Wait! I *do* have something else—pictures."

"Pictures?" he echoed.

"Right. Photographs." She flipped through her wallet, then handed him a well-worn print of a studio portrait. "Me with my mom and stepdad," she announced in triumph. "I was twelve. The picture's a special one. It was taken the day the adoption was final, the day I gained a father and officially became a McKenzie." She smiled.

The girl in the picture looked like her, but . . .

"Photographs can be doctored."

"That one wasn't. And neither was this one." She handed him a snapshot. "My parents and me again. This one was taken at the Toledo airport just before they flew to London."

Teague compared the snapshot with the family portrait. The adults were older but easily recognizable. She was telling the truth. "I'll be damned."

"Probably."

"You really aren't Kirsten, are you?"

"No. I'm not."

At the far end of the carnival grounds, the Tilt-A-Whirl riders screamed in noisy pleasure, their ecstatic squeals punctuated by the staccato bursts of firecrackers in the distance. A chilly little breeze off the lake stirred the pines and raised gooseflesh on Teague's bare arms.

He swatted at a mosquito buzzing hopefully around his head.

"I'm sorry," he said at length. Then, aware of the inadequacy of the apology, he dug his own wallet from his jeans pocket, searched for a particular picture, and passed it to her without another word.

It was a print of a slender, dark-haired girl in shorts and bare feet. She stood poised at the end of a dock against a background of sapphire water and emerald pines. She was laughing into the camera as if she had just pulled off the practical joke of the century.

"It's me," Shea said. "At least it looks like me. Is this Kirsten?"

He nodded.

"No wonder you were so sure I was lying. I'm a dead ringer for her. How spooky."

And under the circumstances, how fortuitous. "Look, Ms. McKenzie, I know now I was way out of line. I realize I must have scared you, and I apologize for that, but . . ." This wasn't going to be easy. How do you tactfully ask someone to assume a false identity?

"But what?"

Oh, hell. "I have a proposition for you. It's a little complicated, though. Why don't we discuss it over coffee?"

Shea stared at him, astonished at his nerve. The man had threatened her, manhandled her, and in general scared her silly. She didn't owe him a damn thing.

"I don't think so."

"Shea?"

It was the first time he'd spoken her name. The echo

of that single soft syllable seemed to shiver down her spine.

Dammit, she couldn't let him get to her. She stared at the ground. "No. My mother always warned me about talking to strangers. I don't even know your name."

"Harris," he said, touching the logo on his tank top. "Teague Harris."

Teague. It suited him. Two little kids raced past, twirling sparklers. In the distance she heard the *pop* of bottle rockets.

"Shea?" He touched her arm and set off a few fireworks of his own.

Startled, she glanced up.

"Please?" The look of entreaty on his face combined with the distraction of his hand on the bare skin of her forearm was more than she could withstand.

"Okay. I'll listen."

He smiled, and Shea's stomach did a freefall.

Oh, brother. What had she let herself in for?

They ended up at the Liberty Lodge Coffee Shop, the only place in town open at that hour. Teague, who'd missed dinner, ordered a cheeseburger and fries. Shea chose the number-three special from the breakfast menu.

"My first impression was right. You are a certifiable nutcase." She shook a forkful of waffle at him, looking eerily like Kirsten from the sweep of her heavy sable lashes to the tempting fullness of her teasing mouth. He wanted . . . Oh, hell. What did it matter what he wanted?

He stabbed a fry with more energy than necessary. "What's so crazy about trying to grant a dying man's wish? Jack Rainey has cancer. His time is running out. All he wants is to see his daughter once more before he dies. Where's the harm in that?"

"Well, for starters, I'm not his daughter. Impersonating an heiress—isn't that fraud or bunco or something?"

He frowned. "It would be if you were trying to profit by it, grab a big inheritance, but this isn't about money."

"No? Then what is it about?"

"I told you. Granting a dying man's wish."

She eyed him skeptically. "You're willing to invest hours in coaching me to impersonate your missing fiancée just to please her father?" She licked whipped cream off the tines of her fork, and the sight of her pink tongue flicking in and out distracted him for a moment.

Kirsten had always picked at her food. Shea ate with obvious enjoyment, so much so that he was about half turned on just watching her. He took a deep breath, trying to remember what they'd been talking about. Oh, yeah. She'd questioned his motivation. Hell, after the way he'd frightened her, the truth was the least he owed her. "When Kirsten disappeared," he said, "it just about killed her father. He paid the ransom, did everything the kidnappers demanded, but he never saw his daughter again. Afterward, he blamed himself for not calling the FBI in sooner.

"Once his younger daughter was born, he seemed to come to terms with his loss. She looks so much like you—" He stopped. "Like Kirsten, I mean." He took a sip of his coffee. "But then when this cancer hit, when he realized he didn't have much time left, Kirsten's disappearance started to prey on his mind again."

The way it had on his. Not a day went by that he didn't think of Kirsten, wonder what had happened to her, wonder who had been responsible for her disappearance and if things might have turned out differently if he hadn't lost his temper the day she told him about the baby.

"But you're right," Teague continued. "I do have another, more selfish reason for wanting you to masquerade as Kirsten." He stared at the window, where moths battered themselves against the glass in a futile attempt to reach the light. Not a bad metaphor for his own existence these last seven years. He'd learned all there was to know about futility, frustration, and shattered dreams.

Shea eyed him warily. "What reason?"

"No one collected the ransom."

She gave him a blank look.

"Don't you get it? No one collected the ransom because she was never really kidnapped. I mean, what's the point of snatching an heiress, demanding a huge ransom, then not picking it up?"

"But—"

He ignored her interruption. "What if sending a ransom note was just a cover-up designed to throw the authorities off the track?"

"Okay, granted that's what happened, what do you think Kirsten's involvement was? Did she run away? Send the ransom note herself?"

"No." Kirsten had been frivolous at times, stubborn and willful frequently, but cruel? Never. She wouldn't have hurt her family by running away. Or him, either. No matter how angry she was.

Murdered. The ugly word remained unspoken, but Teague watched the realization dawn on Shea.

"You think she's dead, don't you?"

He nodded. "It's what I've suspected from the beginning, though I have no proof and no suspect."

She frowned at the remnants of her waffle. "I still don't get it," she said after a pause. "How would my posing as Kirsten help?"

Teague faced her directly. If she agreed to go along with his scheme, she had to know it all. "I want you to help me flush out Kirsten's murderer. I want him to pay."

She tried to pick up her water glass, but her hand was shaking too badly. "So I'm what? The bait? I don't think so." She clenched her hands together. "Besides, what possible good would it do for me to pose as Kirsten? Her murderer, if there is a murderer, would realize right away I'm a fake."

"Yes, but it might shake him up. Rattle him enough, and he's bound to make a mistake."

Shea's crooked little half-smile wasn't meant to be sexy, but that's how his body interpreted it, responding in a way it hadn't for a very long time.

She poked a strawberry. "The problem is, I'd be bound to make a mistake too. I may look like Kirsten, but I don't have her memories. I couldn't fool anyone, particularly not her family."

"You fooled me." He captured her left hand and ran his thumb back and forth across her palm. He felt her shiver slightly in response. "You are Kirsten Rainey down to the last detail."

"Correction." She tugged her fingers free. "I am Shea McKenzie down to the last detail. Shea McKenzie who just happens to resemble Kirsten Rainey."

"To the last detail," he said.

"Even if it is more than a superficial resemblance, I

still couldn't get away with it. We're two different people."

"Don't worry. I can fill you in on whatever background information you need to know. Besides, they'll have no reason to doubt you. They'll dismiss any mistakes you make as memory lapses. You won't be around long enough for anyone besides the murderer to get suspicious."

"You think the murderer is a member of the family?" She bit into the strawberry.

"Someone close to the family, anyway. Someone with inside knowledge."

"That's just great." She shook her head. "Sorry. Not interested."

One thing for sure, she was every damn bit as stubborn as Kirsten. That tongue flicked out again, this time to lick the juice off her lower lip. Teague forced himself to look away.

Another moth smashed into the window with a muffled thump.

Dammit, she could do this. He knew she could.

Teague frowned at her. "If there were just some way I could convince you how important this is . . ." He dug in his wallet for a couple more photographs. Placing them on the table in front of her, he tapped the first snapshot. "This is a picture of Jack and Kirsten taken at Kirsten's engagement party. Can you see the family resemblance?"

Shea put down her fork. She fumbled nervously with the locket that hung from a fine gold chain around her neck.

"And this"—he nudged the second picture—"was taken a few weeks ago. He's gone downhill since." In the second snapshot, Jack Rainey's color was bad. He'd lost a lot of weight.

"You're telling me this man is Kirsten's father?"

He nodded.

Shea shoved her plate aside. She stared at the photographs and Teague stared out the window. Let her think about it awhile. It wasn't an easy decision.

"Teague?"

"Hmm?" He turned to her.

"I probably need my head examined for even considering this," she said, "but I'll do it. Just for a couple of days, I'll be Kirsten."

TWO

Shea returned to her room at the Liberty Lodge just after two A.M. Bone weary but too restless to sleep, she paced the narrow strip of carpet between the end of the bed and the built-in desk and dresser. Her mind reeled with all she'd learned in the last few hours: an apparent kidnapping, a possible murder, an angry fiancé, a grieving father. She worried her locket between thumb and forefinger, seeking comfort from the familiar.

If only she could talk with her mother . . .

She shouldn't have agreed to Teague Harris's crazy scheme. And she wouldn't have if he hadn't shown her the photographs of Kirsten's father.

She'd always known she was illegitimate. According to the story her mother had told her, her father had been killed in Vietnam before he could marry her mother. She'd never questioned that story until now.

Shea flipped open her locket and stared at the only picture she had of her father. Lieutenant John Raines

looked like a younger, healthier version of Jack Rainey.
Coincidence? She wouldn't bet on it.

But if Jack Rainey and John Raines were the same
man, then why had her mother told her that lie about his
dying in southeast Asia? To cover the fact that she'd had
an affair with a married man? Maybe. But that didn't
explain where Elizabeth figured in the equation. *She* was
the one who'd sent the postcard.

Dammit. Shea snapped the locket shut. There were
too many unanswered questions, and she wasn't at all
sure she was going to like the answers. Maybe she should
contact Teague Harris right now and call off the whole
thing before it was too late.

She pulled his card from the back pocket of her
slacks, sat down on the bed, and started to dial. Changing
her mind at the last moment, she broke the connection
before the call had a chance to go through. *Don't be such a
weenie*, she lectured herself. *Are you going to give up on this
the way you gave up on your job?*

She'd worked twelve- and fourteen-hour days—week-
ends and holidays too—as an account executive at the
Plas-Tech Corporation. She certainly hadn't deserved a
pink slip for her efforts. Yet she hadn't said a word in her
own defense, just emptied her desk and walked out.

*Dammit, when will you learn, McKenzie? For once in
your life, fight for what you want. Tackle your difficulties
head-on. Back out now and you'll never know the truth.*

But if she stayed in Liberty . . .

Shea remembered the way Teague's raspy voice had
wrapped itself around her name, the way the hard gray of
his eyes had softened to a smoky charcoal once he realized she wasn't lying, the way her body had responded to

his touch. Tall, dark, and dangerous didn't even begin to cover it.

"Who was Kirsten's best friend in grade school?" Teague asked. He and Shea sat on a rustic bench over-looking the lake. To a casual observer they probably looked like a couple enjoying the scenery and each other. In reality, the park bench was Shea's classroom, Teague her teacher. Neither one of them was interested in the view, and far from enjoying his company, Shea was just about at the end of her tether. When she reached it, she'd probably strangle him with the cord.

"Tamara Johnson," she snapped.

"Johnston," he corrected. "Tamara Johnston."

Shea leaped to her feet. "Johnson? Johnston? Who cares? She moved to Washington at the end of eighth grade. What are the odds the Raineys will drag her into the conversation? No, never mind. I'll tell you what they are. A million to one. This is pointless. You've been grill-ing me for hours, and my poor little brain cells are fried. Isn't it time for recess yet?" Her eyes flashed; her breasts rose and fell with each quick, agitated breath.

Teague stared off across the water toward the island, carefully avoiding both the accusation of the eyes and the temptation of the breasts. *Ought to be a law against those damn sports bras.* Especially under tank tops.

Shea grabbed his hands and dragged him to his feet. "Come on, Teague. Let's play hooky. Just for an hour or two. What do you say?"

Jeez, he was tempted. But he squared his shoulders and tugged his hands free. "I say that in just under twenty-four hours you make your debut appearance as Kirsten Rainey."

"Please, Teague? I'm whipped."

She didn't look whipped. She looked . . . Damn, better not dwell on how she looked. "What was your mother's middle name?"

"Slave driver!"

"Wrong. It was Anne. Elizabeth Anne Lennox Rainey. She died shortly after you were born. Father's middle name?"

"Dammit, Teague."

"Father's middle name?" he repeated.

"I hate you."

"Father's middle name?"

She sank down on the bench in defeat. "Michael," she said with a sigh.

"I'm not ready." Panic engulfed Shea in a suffocating wave. She needed more time. It had been only a week since she'd first agreed to the masquerade. A week of drill and practice as Teague did his best to train her for the role of long-lost daughter. A week of pretending her heart didn't beat out of control every time he looked in her direction.

Teague smiled encouragement. "I've taught you everything I know about Kirsten and her family. You're as ready as you'll ever be. Besides, Jack can't wait forever. When I called yesterday to prepare them for your arrival, Cynthia said he'd had another bad night."

Then Jack Rainey and I have something in common besides our looks.

Massacre Island, the private domain of the Rainey

family, loomed above them like a fortress. It was much larger close up than it had appeared across the lake from the deck of her room at the lodge. Granite ledges shelved up from the water, giving way to a heavy stand of ponderosas. The air was cool and tangy with the scent of the pines. "I'm scared, Teague."

He touched her shoulder briefly, and her heart did a somersault. "Don't be. Just concentrate on what you know. Pop quiz. Describe the family."

"There's Jack, of course, and his second wife, Cynthia."

"Who was . . ." he prompted.

"A widow with a young son Jack later adopted. That's Kevin, now a college student."

"Who else?" Teague cut the motor and they drifted into the mooring at the end of the dock. He used his foot as a bumper, then made fast with the ease of long practice.

"Michaela, Jack and Cynthia's five-year-old daughter, born after Kirsten's disappearance." She stared at the wilderness of rocks and trees. "Where's the house?"

Teague lifted an eyebrow. "You tell me, *Kirsten.*" He held out a hand to help her from the boat.

Ignoring his outstretched fingers, she hopped onto the dock unassisted. Her brain was barely functioning as it was. If he touched her again, the few remaining circuits would short out for sure. "Straight along the path to the south side of the island. Do not pass Go. Do not collect two hundred dollars," she recited. "I've got the directions memorized. I just thought we ought to be able to see the house from here."

"Too many trees in the way." He squeezed her hand, and her spine melted.

"I can't do this," she said, not sure whether she was talking about meeting the Rainey family or pretending to be his fiancée.

"Yes, you can." His voice was low and soothing. "Think positively." He nodded toward the path. "The welcoming committee just cleared the trees. Follow my lead." He pulled her into an embrace and kissed her with more enthusiasm than she felt the situation merited. Dammit, she was shaky enough without having to deal with a hormone rush.

"Don't lose yourself in the part," she warned through her teeth while gazing adoringly up into his face.

His answering smile made her tremble. "Who says I'm acting?" He kept one arm draped around her as they turned to greet the others. "Cynthia, Kevin, Mikey—look who's back."

Shea fought to still her trembling and concentrate on the Raineys.

Kirsten's stepmother approached first, an attractive woman as slim and chic at forty-four as most women half her age. She pulled Shea into a welcoming hug, enveloping her in warmth and Chanel No. 5. "Kirsten," she said in a shaky voice, "I can't believe you're here. I never thought we'd see you again. It's wonderful to have you home." Tears glistened in her eyes. She released Shea and pulled her son and daughter closer. "Say hello to your sister."

Fair-haired, blue-eyed Kevin, a nineteen-year-old sophomore at the University of Idaho, was startlingly handsome with near-perfect features. He took Shea's hand in a firm grip, then pulled her close. "It's good to have you back, Kirsten," he whispered in her ear. "We've missed you."

When he let her go, she smiled up at him. "I missed you too, Skeeter."

An odd expression rippled across his surface composure. He wasn't trembling on the brink of tears like Cynthia, yet it was obvious that this meeting was affecting him as profoundly as it was his mother. "I'd almost forgotten that old nickname. I must have been a rotten little pest."

She grinned. "Rotten maybe. Pest definitely. But little? Never."

Teague shot her a questioning look, a slight frown marring his forehead. Had she messed up already?

Kevin shoved his little half sister forward. "Say hello to Kirsten, Mikey."

Michaela Rainey was the image of Shea at five. She had the same straight little nose, clear blue-green eyes, tousled dark ringlets, and stubbornly squared-off chin with just the hint of a cleft. Right now the chin was thrust forward aggressively, her lower lip in pouting mode.

She stood toe-to-toe with Shea. "You're not my sister. My sister's dead. Ruth said so and *she* doesn't lie."

Cynthia gasped. "Mikey, you're being rude." She dragged her daughter away from Shea. "Apologize to Kirsten this instant."

"I won't!" A mutinous expression twisted the little girl's features. "She's not Kirsten. She's a nimposter who's trying to steal our island."

"Michaela Rainey, apologize at once." Cynthia's expression was thunderous.

The child twisted loose. "I won't! And you can't make me." Then she turned on her heel and took off up the path.

Cynthia looked as if she were about to follow, but

Kevin placed a restraining hand on her arm. "Let her go," he said. "It's not her fault. Ruth has been filling her head full of that garbage for years." Kevin glanced at Shea. "You remember our beloved housekeeper?"

"Does she still whistle 'Rock of Ages' for hours on end?"

Kevin grimaced. "Her musical shortcomings are the least of the problem. A few years ago she joined a very strict sect called the Tabernacle of the Blessed. If you thought she had a weird take on religion before, you should hear her now. She's got those two kids of hers on their knees every five minutes praying for forgiveness for some imagined sin or other."

"If she's gone off the deep end," Teague said, "why not fire her?"

"Jack won't hear of it." Cynthia frowned. "And he has a point. Ruth's been a fixture on Massacre Island longer than I have. Besides, she's an excellent house-keeper as well as a trained nurse. I don't know how I'd manage Jack's care without her." She turned to Shea. "Teague explained about your amnesia." Her smile was so sympathetic, Shea felt like a worm for deceiving her.

"Yes, my memory is still pretty patchy."

Teague wrapped an arm around her shoulders. She glanced up, surprising an expression on his face that made her feel dizzy. All week, during the incessant drills in Rainey family minutiae, he'd kept a careful emotional distance. He'd been by turns a bully, a buddy, and a brother. She'd decided all the heavy-duty sexual aware-ness was one-sided. Evidently, she'd decided wrong. The fierce, tender yearning of his expression told her that. She shivered in reaction, then frowned as another possi-bility occurred to her. Was it she he wanted? Or Kirsten?

Thankfully, conversation was sporadic as they took the path to the house. Shea found it difficult to think with Teague's arm around her.

The scenery was gorgeous, the views increasingly spectacular as they climbed toward the crest of the island. They paused at the top to catch their breath and appreciate the dramatic vista down the length of Crescent Lake.

"This is where the lookout was posted back in pioneer days. Can you imagine how young David Rainey must have felt when he woke up—he'd fallen asleep at his post," Kevin explained for Teague's benefit, "and saw Indians approaching in war canoes?"

"White men dressed as Indians," Shea said. "Thugs hired by Angus Fitzhugh, a local land baron who coveted the island."

Teague shot her a funny look. That wasn't a topic his coaching had covered.

Kevin smiled approval. He'd been testing her and she'd just aced the final exam. "The massacre, the one that gives the island its name—"

"It's a grisly name," Cynthia Rainey said with a shudder of distaste.

"—killed off the entire Rainey family except for David, the boy who fell asleep on guard duty. Imagine the guilt of knowing you were responsible for the slaughter of your entire family." Kevin's eyes held a challenge. The earlier test hadn't been the final exam after all.

"Hardly." Shea gave him her blandest smile. "Even if David had given the alarm in time, the result would have been the same. The Raineys were grossly outnumbered. The only difference was that since David lived to tell the tale, the Indians weren't blamed for something they didn't do and that greedy Fitzhugh got what he deserved." She'd always been a straight-A student.

"If you two are done arguing the fine points of family history," Cynthia said with an indulgent smile, "Jack's waiting. I suggest we head on down to the house."

"Second that motion." Teague shot Shea a sharp glance.

The path continued downhill through the trees, then emerged into a small meadow ablaze with wildflowers—purple delphiniums, yellow daisies, giant red paintbrushes, and the delicate white lace of wild parsley. A black and yellow helicopter perched on a cement pad in the center of the clearing like a giant mutated bumblebee. Beyond the meadow another band of trees—ponderosas, lodgepole pines, hemlock, and alders—sheltered the house and grounds.

The house shouldn't have surprised her. She knew the Raineys were rich, but Teague had thrown her off by referring to the place as "the family's summer cabin." To her, cabin meant small and rustic, not an enormous two-story complex big enough to be mistaken for a hotel. A multilevel deck connected the main living spaces and surrounded the Olympic-size pool on three sides. The only way in which it coincided with Shea's concept of a cabin was the fact that it was constructed of logs.

Shea and Teague were left alone on the deck while Cynthia went to find out if Jack was ready to see Kirsten and Kevin checked on lunch. Presumably, Mikey was still off sulking.

Teague turned Shea to face him. "So tell me, *Kirsten*, how did you know about David Rainey and the evil land baron?"

She narrowed her eyes. "The name's Shea."

"Is it? Then explain where you heard about the massacre."

"I read the story in a brochure I picked up in the lobby of the Liberty Lodge." Was he really having doubts about her identity at this late date? Or was it just wishful thinking on his part?

He studied her unsmilingly. "How did you know Kirsten's nickname for Kevin?"

She blinked. How *had* she known? "You must have told me."

"Uh-uh." He shook his head. "First I heard of it was today."

"Then maybe I got it from the diaries you had me read." Kirsten's diaries. She wondered for the first time how they'd come into his possession.

"Maybe, though I don't recall ever reading the name Skeeter." He nodded thoughtfully. "Maybe I skimmed over that part."

He hadn't. The nickname wasn't mentioned anywhere in the diaries she'd all but memorized. So how *had* she known? Shea had no clue. Tiny hairs raised along her arms. She couldn't meet Teague's gaze.

"You threw me for a minute," he said.

She nodded. "Like Kevin almost threw me. I've been lucky so far, but I'm never going to be able to pull this off. Sooner or later I'm going to make a major blunder."

He encircled her wrist in a gesture meant to be reassuring. Instead, it set her skin on fire, her nerves so sensitive to his touch that she could almost feel the individual ridges on the pads of his fingers, pressing against her pulse point.

"You'll do fine," he said. "If you make a mistake, just fall back on your cover story. The kidnappers got a little too rough and you ended up with a concussion. Panicky, scared you were going to die, they abandoned you in a hospital emergency room halfway across the country."

She frowned, trying to ignore the sudden heat his touch ignited. Her breasts felt tight and heavy, her legs shaky. *Concentrate on the cover story*, she told herself, but it was hopeless. The gentle pressure of his fingers on her wrist distracted her, and she couldn't help wondering how it would feel to have that same gentle pressure caressing other, more intimate portions of her anatomy.

"And when you finally regained consciousness . . ." he prompted, releasing her wrist.

She loosed her pent-up breath in a long sigh. One by one her fried brain cells came back on line. "I had amnesia," she said. "For years, I've been having little flickers of memory, one of which brought me to Liberty in search of a clue to my past. When I ran into you, whole chunks of my previous life came into focus."

"Though you still have a few gaps." He leaned forward and kissed her lightly.

An incredible rush of emotion flooded her, so intense she nearly fainted. The kiss, a mere brush of his lips, lasted only a second, but when he stepped back, Shea was completely disoriented, a tangled skein of nerve endings, all of which were throbbing.

"Ready?" he asked.

Oh, my, yes. She'd never been more ready in her life.

"Here comes Cynthia," he whispered.

"What?"

"To take you inside to see Jack."

"Right. Jack."

Teague shot her a worried look. "Are you okay?"

"Fine," she lied. Jeez, what was wrong with her?

She'd always been such a cool, controlled person. When had her sex drive suddenly started this wild race down the fast lane? *Concentrate. You're about to meet a man who may prove to be your father.*

Cynthia approached, a smile on her face. "Your father's waiting, Kirsten. He wants to see you too, Teague."

"Teague?" Shea echoed in surprise. She tensed. Had Jack Rainey seen through their pretense already? Was the world about to fall down around their ears?

Teague slid an arm around her waist. "Don't worry," he said. "It'll be all right." Easy for him to say. He wasn't the one who'd end up in prison for impersonating an heiress.

He steered her toward a set of sliding glass doors. Shea's legs felt like overcooked asparagus.

Inside the house, she regained her equilibrium along with her bearings. Second door on the right, she remembered, in what used to be the library until Jack got too frail to climb the stairs. The faint lemony scent of furniture polish seemed familiar. She wondered if her Nancy Drew collection still occupied the bottom shelf.

Cynthia had left the door ajar. Teague knocked. "Jack?"

"Teague? Is Kirsten with you?" His voice was more powerful than she'd expected.

But as they stepped across the threshold, she realized Jack Rainey's strong baritone was misleading. Teague hadn't been exaggerating when he said the man wouldn't be able to wait forever. He looked like a man on borrowed time.

Kirsten's father was skeletally thin, the pale, sallow skin of his face hanging from the bony framework of his skull. Only his eyes seemed alive. The exact same aquamarine shade as Shea's, they burned with a passion for life. Cancer wasn't taking Jack Rainey without a fight.

Stepping around the IV bag dripping glucose and morphine into his veins, Shea moved closer to the bed. "Daddy?"

One of the waxen claws on the coverlet twitched in a silent request. Shea edged closer and cradled the claw between her hands. His skin was hot and dry, as if he were burning up from the inside out. "Oh, Daddy," she said.

"I thought I'd never see you again. Thank God Teague found you." His voice shook with emotion. The claw moved feebly in her hands. "Don't cry, baby."

Shea realized with a shock that tears were sliding down her cheeks. "Sorry. I can't help it."

Teague gave her shoulder a squeeze. "How are you today?" he asked Jack.

Jack's smile was ironic. "I've been better. Though it's a load off my mind to see the two of you together again. All these years I've blamed myself."

"Oh, Daddy, no," she protested. "Why blame yourself? You did everything humanly possible. Teague told me you followed the kidnapper's instructions down to the last detail. You kept the police out of it and paid the ransom. What more could you have done?"

He fell silent for a moment, then turned a gaunt, hollow-eyed look on Teague. "She doesn't remember, does she?"

Shea felt a stirring of uneasiness. "Remember what?"

Teague shook his head. "I didn't mention it. I figured she had enough to assimilate as it was."

Jack Rainey's papery eyelids fell shut, concealing his

fierce, glowing eyes. He looked like a corpse. A deep sigh rattled his chest. "You should have told her."

She turned to Teague. "Told me what?"

Shrugging, he refused to meet her gaze.

She swung around to face Jack again. His eyes were open now, dispelling the illusion of death. "What, Daddy? Tell me."

"You remember how fiercely I opposed your engagement?"

She shook her head. "Only what Teague told me. That part's still a blur. Teague said I had to threaten to elope before you'd agree to let me marry him. You thought he was a fortune hunter."

Jack shut his eyes again for a moment. "I was wrong about that. I was wrong about a lot of things." Slowly he lifted his lids to reveal eyes that blazed with intensity. "But you didn't just threaten to elope, Kirsten. You did elope. You and Teague are married, have been for the last seven years."

Shea's cheeks burned. "But Teague said I disappeared two days *before* the wedding."

"Before the big, fancy public wedding I pressed for. The after-the-fact cover-up my pride demanded. By God, I insisted, nobody was going to look down his nose at a Rainey. I was able to keep the elopement secret from everyone but the immediate family." A faint smile touched his lips. "Even from Ruth."

She frowned. "That doesn't explain why you fault yourself. Just because you insisted on a formal ceremony?"

Teague spoke up. "He blames himself because the wedding's what you and I fought over, why you moved back home."

"Where you fell right into the kidnapper's trap. I did everything but bait it for him." Jack sounded tired. Dead tired.

Teague took a step toward the bed. "That's enough. You need some rest."

Jack moved fretfully against the pillows. "But she doesn't remember."

Shea took his hands in hers. "It's okay, Daddy. All that was a long time ago. Water under the bridge. Get some rest now. We'll talk again later."

He heaved a sigh. "Promise?"

"Cross my heart."

"Good. There are things that need to be said," he muttered, and fell into an uneasy doze.

Lunch was finished, but Shea, Teague, Kevin, and Cynthia lingered at the umbrella-shaded table on the deck, sipping iced tea and talking in a desultory fashion while Glory and Hallelujah, the housekeeper's twins, cleared away the remains of the meal.

"Have you seen your room yet?" Cynthia asked Shea. "No? It's just as you left it. Your father always insisted that you'd find your way back home someday."

"I'll take her up," Kevin offered. "Who has the key?"

"The key?" Shea asked.

"Your room is kept locked," Cynthia explained. "Another of your father's quirks."

"Mama has the key," Glory said, studying her sturdy brown oxfords as if their scuff marks were hieroglyphics that, once deciphered, might unlock the secrets of the universe. It was the first time she'd spoken all day, and Shea couldn't have been any more surprised if the log wall behind her had suddenly started spouting poetry. "Soon as I finish clearing the table, I'll get it."

"Hal can finish up here," Kevin said. "Run and get the key now."

Glory flicked a sideways glance at Kevin, flushed bright pink, and scuttled off.

So it's that way, is it? Shea thought. Well, no wonder. Kevin was the walking embodiment of Prince Charming. Unfortunately, with her mousy hair, baby fat, and overbite, Glory was no Sleeping Beauty.

"Kevin, for heaven's sake," Cynthia objected, "the twins are not your personal slaves."

"Glory doesn't mind, and Hal doesn't, either. Do you, Hal?"

The boy shook his head and continued piling dirty dishes on a tray. Rail thin with lank hair, dandruff, and acne, he was an even less prepossessing specimen than his sister.

"Mind if I tag along?" Teague asked. "I've never seen your room. Maybe it'll give me fresh insights into your personality."

"Or Cynthia's," Shea said. "She did the decorating." She felt a prickling of unease. And how did she know that? Had someone mentioned it earlier?

Glory came bustling back out with the key just then, ready to lead them upstairs, so Shea gave the matter no more thought.

Kirsten's room was like a page out of *Country Living*, picture perfect from the framed Wooster Scott primitives clustered on the wall between the dormer windows to the antique spool bed with its red and white patchwork quilt.

"Whoa. Time warp." Laughing, Teague grabbed his picture from the bedside table and passed it to Shea. "My long hair period, one of many reasons your father hated my guts."

Seven years ago, he'd have been what? Twenty-five to Kirsten's nineteen? The man in the picture looked even younger. More than Teague's haircut had changed.

"Where did this come from?" Kevin held up a crystal cluster. It caught the light in a dazzling blue-green flash.

Fascinated, Shea moved closer to run a finger along one smooth facet. The stone felt warm, and if she hadn't known better, she'd have sworn it vibrated beneath her fingertip.

She gazed into the heart of the stone, blinded by a sudden dazzle. A low, throbbing hum filled her ears and something powerful stirred just below the level of conscious thought. Images zigzagged through her brain at lightning speed, too fast to comprehend, too vivid to ignore, in a rushing montage that was there and then gone so fast she might have imagined it. She blinked and jerked her hand away.

Frowning, Kevin put the crystal back on the nightstand, where he'd found it. "I know I would have noticed if the crystal had been here before."

"It's one of Beelzebub's treasures. He dragged it in the house a couple months back. I probably should have tossed it out, but the color reminded me of your eyes, Miss Kirsten." Glory seemed nervous, staring everywhere but at the crystal. Perhaps she was worried that she'd broken one of her mother's rules or maybe she was just embarrassed at her own temerity in speaking up.

"Who's Beelzebub?" Shea asked. If Teague had mentioned that name, she'd have remembered.

"Mikey's black Lab," Kevin explained. "The canine pack rat."

Teague picked up the crystal cluster to examine it more closely.

Shea stared at the stone, afraid to touch it a second time but unable to look away. The carnival Gypsy's words seemed to echo in her ears. *The secret's in the stone.*

What secret? she wondered. Something to do with the way the crystal's many facets reflected her face over and over again? If she were a fanciful woman, she might almost think there was another Shea trapped inside the crystal, looking out.

"Kirsten?" Teague touched her shoulder.

"What?" She tore her gaze away from the myriad reflections of her own frightened expression to focus on his face.

Worry wrinkled his brow. "Are you all right?" he asked.

"Fine." She forced a smile. "A little tired," she said, though "a little scared" was closer to the truth. She didn't like the way memories kept surfacing. It wasn't natural. How could she remember things she'd never known in the first place?

THREE

Shea looked depressed, despite the fact that her visit with the Raineys had gone like clockwork. "Problem?" Teague asked as they pulled away from the island.

She frowned. "Why didn't you tell me you and Kirsten had eloped?"

"I was afraid you'd start seeing ulterior motives in everything I said or did, and besides, it's not something I'm especially proud of."

"Why? You didn't marry her for her money, did you?"

"No." He was silent for a moment. "It's a long story, Shea. Sure you want to hear it?"

"Under the circumstances, I think it would be best," she said dryly.

Best for whom? Teague wondered. Not him. It was a subject he tried not to dwell on, though right after Kirsten's disappearance, he hadn't been able to think of anything else. For a while his only refuge from the pain of those memories had been at the bottom of a beer bottle.

He hadn't gotten his life back on track for almost a year. And without Jack Rainey's help, he might never have made it at all. He owed Jack. And if baring his soul to Shea would help pay that debt, then so be it.

"Kirsten's mother died when she was a baby. And until she was eleven—that's when Jack married Cynthia—she had her father to herself. He adored her and pretty much gave her whatever she wanted. Don't get me wrong. Kirsten adored her father too, but she wasn't above using his love for her to get her own way."

"Spoiled and headstrong," Shea translated.

Teague nodded. "But also charming and lovable. I think when her father refused to sanction her marriage to me, it must have been the first time he'd ever told her no."

"But she didn't take no for an answer?"

He shook his head. "She *never* took no for an answer. Kirsten knew her father's pride was his greatest weakness, and she used it against him. She knew if she eloped, he would agree to the big wedding she wanted as a face-saving measure."

"And you went along with the plan to manipulate her father?"

"I didn't realize what she was planning. All I knew was that I wanted to marry Kirsten, and eloping seemed to be the only option."

Shea looked puzzled. "But if her father was that opposed to the match, then why did he give in? So you eloped. Big deal. Why not arrange an annulment or a quiet divorce?"

Teague stared back at the green hump of Massacre Island. "His pride wouldn't allow that, not once she told him she was pregnant."

"Pregnant?" She choked on the word. "Is that what Jack wanted to talk to me about?"

"Probably." He clenched his hand on the rudder. "That baby was Kirsten's ace in the hole. In the end, it's what forced him to cave in to her demand for a big wedding. She knew her father so well, knew that from Jack's perspective a bastard grandchild was a thousand times worse than a fortune-hunting son-in-law."

"You weren't really a fortune hunter, though."

"No, I was crazy in love with her." He laughed sourly. "Or maybe just crazy. I'd never met anyone like Kirsten before. She was intelligent, wealthy, and beautiful. Most women like that are so impressed with their own perfection, they set themselves apart from lesser mortals. Kirsten was different. She loved life, loved people. She'd run errands for housebound senior citizens, tutor kids with reading disabilities, volunteer to baby-sit a colicky baby, or sit with an AIDS patient. And anyone who was special to her earned a pet nickname."

"Like Skeeter," she said.

He nodded. "Despite the age difference, Kevin and Kirsten were very close. Closer than many blood siblings."

"I wouldn't know about that. I'm an only child."

"Me too," he said as he maneuvered the boat into its berth in the boathouse at Strawberry Point.

"The Raineys own this boathouse too?"

Teague nodded. "The Griffins live in the apartment above the one on the island. I live here. Want to take a look around before I drive you back to the lodge?" The real Kirsten would have made herself at home, conned him into fixing her dinner, then seduced him over dessert.

Shea's gaze locked with his. Her color rose as if she'd read his mind. Then she shook her head, breaking off eye contact. "Give me a raincheck."

"Sure." Her blush proved she wasn't completely indifferent to him. Good news, since he was far from indifferent to her.

And it wasn't, he told himself, as they drove back along the lake to Liberty, just because she looked like Kirsten. After spending a week in Shea's company, he recognized the differences between the two. Both were bright and stubborn as hell, but Kirsten had been manipulative where Shea was not.

Shea was more independent too. Kirsten had had no interest in furthering her education or doing anything beyond charity work. Shea, on the other hand, had worked her way through college and built a career in the corporate world. In *Ohio*, he reminded himself. And she wasn't the type to abandon all her hard-earned junior-executive perks to follow a man, either. Especially not a man who was still struggling to get his own fledgling business off the ground. Teague sighed.

There were other differences too. Kirsten had been a born flirt. She'd known all the courtship rituals by heart and practiced them religiously. By contrast, Shea didn't play any games at all.

And though he could tell she was attracted to him, she wasn't the type of woman to accept a man at face value. Kirsten had been as open and trusting as a puppy, but Shea hadn't made up her mind about him yet. Teague understood, even approved of, her wariness. Trust didn't come easily for him, either.

He pulled into the parking lot of the Liberty Lodge, removed his sunglasses, and tucked them above the visor.

"I know the big reunion was hard on you, but seeing his 'daughter' again did Jack a world of good. When I spoke to him after lunch, he seemed better than he has been in weeks."

"That's good," she said to the dashboard.

"Shea?"

She looked at him. Her expression was neutral, but she was as aware of him as he was of her. Little things gave her away—the faint flush along her cheekbones, the increase in her respiration rate, the way she twisted her purse strap between her fingers. A strand of hair had worked loose from the ponytail at the nape of her neck. He was tempted to hook it back behind her ear. Any excuse to touch her. But he didn't. He smiled instead.

Shea's color rose and she broke off eye contact. "Cynthia asked me to come back in the morning. She thought going through old pictures might help to restore the gaps in my memory."

"You don't have to go back if you don't want to. Jack's seen you now. His mind's at rest. I can fob her off with some story. I'll be out there tomorrow anyway. My crew and I are scheduled to start work on a new project."

"No, I . . ." She flushed. "Cynthia's expecting me." She met his gaze. "Tell me about your project. It's a landscaping job, I take it?"

"There's an old gazebo on the promontory, used to be Kirsten's favorite spot on the island, but the trees and shrubs have grown so tall, they've blocked the view. Jack got it in his head that he had to restore the spot to its former glory. He hired us to clear out brush, add some plantings, put in a brick path."

"So you'll be on Massacre Island all day?"

"Most of it. I can take you over in the morning if you

want. Or, better yet, why don't I show you how to run an outboard? Then you can take yourself across whenever you feel like it."

"That makes sense."

A freckle-faced girl with carroty hair scooted past on a skateboard. When Shea turned to watch, Teague studied her profile: perfect nose, full lower lip, stubborn chin. He wanted to touch her. Hell, he wanted to drag her into his arms and kiss her until she was breathless and panting his name, but he didn't have the right. She wasn't really Kirsten. She wasn't really his at all.

Shea turned back to him. "When can you show me how to run the boat motor?"

He glanced at his watch. "I have a few errands, but I can swing back by to pick you up about seven. That would give us a couple hours of daylight to mess with the boat."

"Sure."

She didn't look sure, but she didn't turn him down, either, which, he figured, qualified as a step in the right direction. His direction.

With mixed feelings, Shea watched Teague's pickup drive off. The man was tall, dark, and growing more dangerous by the minute. He smiled and her brain shorted out. He touched and her hormones went berserk. What had she let herself in for?

Inside the lodge's rustic lobby, the desk clerk handed over her key, then placed an envelope on the counter in front of her. "This came for you."

Shea took the letter, then turned it over to study the typewritten address. Despite the fact that no one back home knew where she was, the letter was addressed to Ms. Shea McKenzie in care of the lodge. She frowned. Who could be sending her letters?

The return address was conspicuous by its absence. She checked the postmark. It had been mailed locally, which told her—what?

"Thanks," she told the desk clerk, stuffing the envelope into her purse. She left by a side door and took the path along the lake.

Most of the guests were out on the water or enjoying the lodge's recreational facilities. The grounds were almost deserted. She met no one on the way to her room except for a family of quail, mama and babies, marching down the shredded-bark path in a straggling line.

The phone was ringing as she let herself into her room. She tossed her jacket on the bed and grabbed the receiver. "Hello?"

There was no response at first, though she could hear someone breathing. *Oh, great. A crank call. Just what I need.*

"Hello?" she tried again, louder this time.

"Go back to where you came from." The voice on the other end was as dry and whispery as dead leaves rustling in the wind.

"Who is this?"

"A friend. Did you get your mail?"

"Who *is* this?"

No answer. The line was dead.

She hung up the phone with trembling fingers, then dug in her purse for the letter the desk clerk had given her. She ripped it open to find a yellowed newspaper clipping and a single page of white bond.

The clipping was a brief account of Kirsten's disappearance. The accompanying note was typed. Its author hadn't believed in wasting words. Its message was short, if not sweet:

History has a way of repeating itself.

Shea huddled in a wingback chair, toying with her locket. The whispering voice on the phone had claimed to be a friend, though he—or she—hadn't sounded particularly friendly. She fingered the clipping. According to the article, Kirsten Rainey had disappeared without a trace, and the FBI reported no new leads. Nothing there she hadn't already known. Which brought her to the note itself. *History has a way of repeating itself.* Warning or threat? That's what she couldn't decide.

Dammit, she needed to talk to her mom. Only she couldn't. Her parents weren't due home for another three weeks. And it wasn't as if they were on a group tour with a planned itinerary. Shea knew they intended to spend some time in Scotland trying to trace her stepdad's ancestors. And she also knew her mom was determined to visit Pompeii. But as to when they'd be where, she had no clue. They probably didn't know themselves.

Shea jumped nervously at a tap on the door. Teague already? She glanced at her watch, surprised to discover that it had been forty minutes since he'd dropped her off.

She frowned, debating with herself whether or not to tell him about the unsettling crank call and anonymous note. Too risky, she decided. What if he insisted on calling off the charade? She wasn't ready to leave Liberty yet, not until she had the answers to a few questions of her own.

Stuffing the note and the news clipping in her purse, she got up to let him in.

"What's wrong?" he asked as soon as he saw her face.

"Nothing. I'm just hungry. I was too nervous to eat much at lunch."

He glanced at his watch. "Want to go grab something before class?"

"Class?"

"You remember. Boating 101."

She forced a smile. "I vote for class first, then food."

Teague looked puzzled. "But a second ago you said you were hungry."

"Let's just say I'm a big proponent of delayed gratification. You know, the longer you wait, the more you appreciate it." Which might be mistaken for sexual innuendo, though she hadn't meant it that way. Shea's cheeks grew warm. "Shall we go?"

Teague raised an eyebrow. "Whenever you're ready."

"Not bad." Teague nodded approval. "Just remember not to come roaring up to the dock full throttle. You don't want to skin up the boat. Or the dock, either." He gave her shoulder a squeeze when she brought the little Seaswirl gliding in next to the mooring. "Yeah, I think you're getting the hang of it."

"Finally." Shea grinned and a dimple flashed in her right cheek.

Kirsten had had an identical dimple.

"What is it?" she asked, and he realized he'd been staring.

"You look so damn much like her. It can't be coincidence. Somewhere along the line you must have Rainey blood."

"Not that I'm aware of. You know what they say. Everyone has a double somewhere in the world. I guess I just happen to be Kirsten's."

Her explanation was a little too glib. Her gaze slid away from his.

Shea McKenzie was hiding something. He'd bet a month's income on it. She wasn't Kirsten, but she had some connection with the Raineys. With Jack.

It wasn't, he remembered, until after he'd shown her the pictures of Jack that she'd agreed to impersonate Kirsten. At the time he'd thought compassion for a dying man had sparked her sudden change of heart. But what if compassion hadn't been the motivating factor? What if seeing Jack's photographs had stirred a darker emotion?

Who was Shea McKenzie, anyway? An illegitimate daughter? One Jack didn't even know about? If so, maybe her presence in Liberty wasn't a coincidence, after all. *Maybe she's after the money.* The nasty suspicion slithered through his head, poisoning his thoughts.

Dammit. Had he been paying more attention to his hormones than his common sense? A smart man would have asked Sheriff Carlton to run a discreet background check on Ms. Shea McKenzie a week ago when she first turned up. And maybe *he'd* do that too. First thing tomorrow.

Teague stepped onto the dock, stretching out a hand to help Shea. Her fingers were warm, her palm a little moist, as if she was uneasy, as if he made her uneasy. She glanced up at him with a nervous smile. "Thanks," she said, her voice a breathless whisper.

Oh, hell. First thing tomorrow. Tomorrow afternoon. The day after.

He thought about kissing her, dragging her down on the worn boards of the dock and kissing her long and hard until she was as sick and dizzy with wanting as he was.

Had she read his mind? A flicker of fear lit those pale Rainey eyes. And unless he was mistaken, a flicker of excitement too.

Neither of them spoke. Water lapped against the pilings. A breeze rustled through the pines. Out on the lake a trout broke the surface with a plop. In the gathering dusk, Shea's skin looked pale, almost luminous against the backdrop of trees and water. She would feel like silk against the roughness of his callused palms. Feel like silk and taste like honey.

He wanted her. God, but he wanted her. Her warm, spicy scent teased his senses. She was so close, close enough to touch. All he had to do was . . .

A mosquito whined past his ear, then nailed him on the forearm. He swatted at it, and the prosaic action snapped the thread of heightened awareness linking them. He frowned at the dark hump of Massacre Island in the distance. Damn, what was his problem? He was thirty-two years old, for crying out loud, not some horny teenager.

Turning abruptly, he led the way to the boathouse and showed her where the extra key was kept. "Just in case you need to use a boat sometime when they're all put away. Hungry?" he asked without making eye contact.

"Starved." She sounded so normal, so unconcerned,

he glanced over at her. Had he imagined that golden moment on the dock?

"We could run into Liberty, grab a pizza or something, or you could cash in that raincheck. I do a mean omelet," he said.

She smiled an innocent, let's-be-friends smile, but her lower lip trembled just a little. "Right now I'm so hungry I'd accept a dinner invitation from the devil himself."

That's right, he told himself. *Keep it light. Keep it casual.* He lifted an eyebrow. "I suppose you know that remark just earned you the dishwashing detail, McKenzie."

She hadn't been kidding about being hungry, he thought as he watched her polish off the last of her omelet and a second roll, then eye the apple pie with a predatory expression. "You're definitely not Kirsten," he said.

"So I've said. Repeatedly. What finally convinced you?"

"Kirsten ate like a bird, was always on a diet, always worrying about her weight. She used to irritate the hell out of me. We'd go out to dinner and she'd order the most expensive thing on the menu, eat two bites, then say she was full. You, on the other hand, take a much less inhibited approach to food."

She laid down her fork and studied him from between narrowed lids. "Meaning what? I suck it in like a vacuum cleaner?"

He laughed at the outraged expression on her face. "Relax. It was a compliment, not an insult."

"Oh," she said, her cheeks turning a delicate pink.

"Got room for some pie?"

Her eyes sparkled and her lips curved in a smile. "Yes, please."

He cut her a generous piece.

She paused, the first bite just inches from her mouth. "Aren't you having any?"

The truth was, he'd rather watch her eat. She did it with such gusto, such obvious pleasure. "Maybe later," he said. "I had more lunch than you did."

She nodded, then closed her eyes as she savored the taste.

"I couldn't eat. That visit was so nerve-racking. It didn't help to have Ruth Griffin glaring at me through the entire meal as if she thought I might slip poison into someone's food."

"She'll warm up. Give her time."

Teague watched in fascination as she licked a flake of crust off her fork. Before meeting Shea, he hadn't realized what a turn-on it could be just watching a woman eat.

"Teague?"

"Hmm?"

"Do you believe in ghosts?"

He laughed in surprise. Ghosts? Talk about your non sequiturs. What was going on in that head of hers? "No. I think when you're dead, you're dead, and that's it. Finito. Caput. The end. Why do you ask?"

She stabbed a slice of apple as if she had a grudge against it. "I know this sounds crazy, but today, out on the island, a couple of times I knew things I shouldn't have. Like somebody was filtering information into my brain."

He studied her face closely. Was she setting him up for some con? "Give me an example."

She cocked her head to one side. "Like when I knew Cynthia had decorated Kirsten's room."

"Decorating is what Cynthia does best. In the fifteen years or so she and Jack have been married, she's redecorated the cabin at least four times. I probably mentioned something about it when I briefed you on the family."

"That's my point. I don't remember your touching on the subject." She frowned slightly, biting her lip. "I don't know, though. Maybe you did." She didn't sound convinced.

"Okay, what's *your* theory? That Kirsten's haunting you? Planting her memories in your brain?"

"I told you it sounded crazy."

"Not crazy, exactly."

She squared her jaw and pressed her lips together in a firm line. "Don't patronize me, dammit. I know it sounds nuts, but I also know I'm not imagining all the weird little anomalies. There have been too damn many of them for coincidence."

"Such as?"

"Such as how did I know Kirsten called Kevin 'Skeeter'? The nickname wasn't mentioned in the diaries. I'm positive. And later, when we went to see Jack, I 'remembered' where Kirsten's old Nancy Drew collection was shelved. Not to mention . . ." Her eyes glazed over as if she were listening intently to the murmur of distant voices.

"What?" The fey expression on her face made him nervous.

"The crystal." She shivered, even though the room was warm.

"The aquamarine cluster in Kirsten's room?"

She nodded.

"What about it?"

Shea frowned at a spot on the wall just over his left shoulder. "I'm not sure. But when I touched it, I had the eeriest sensation. A communication, I think, but it came so fast, I couldn't make sense of it."

"In that case, you can count Kirsten out. According to Glory, the rock's one of Beelzebub's treasures. No connection to Kirsten at all."

"There's a connection," she said flatly. "You didn't feel what I felt."

Teague took her hand between his. She vibrated with tension. Bizarre as her ideas sounded to him, she believed what she was saying. "If it bothers you that much to visit the island, don't go back."

"But I have to." She tugged her hand free of his grasp and faced him directly. "Teague, are you absolutely certain that Kirsten's dead?"

The pain had dulled to an ache over the years, but it still bothered him to talk about Kirsten's disappearance. "Ninety-nine percent sure."

"So who killed her? And why? You must have a theory."

"Theories, yes. Proof, no." He shoved his chair back and gripped the edge of the table so hard, the tips of his fingers looked white.

"Whom do you suspect?"

"Nobody. Everybody." He shook his head. "The world is full of sickos."

She put down her fork and shoved the pie plate away. "Since you brought up sickos, how about Ruth Griffin as a suspect? She's definitely unbalanced."

"In her own way, Ruth cared for Kirsten. She didn't approve of everything Kirsten did, but she loved her anyway."

"Maybe loved her to death."

"But—"

"No, just listen for a second." Shea cut off his protest. "If Ruth thought Kirsten was doing something that put her immortal soul in danger, Ruth might see murder as a way of 'saving' her."

In a twisted way, it made sense. "Maybe," he admitted, "but to my mind, Cynthia had a better motive."

Shea looked skeptical. "Somehow she doesn't strike me as the evil stepmother type."

Teague shrugged. He'd never cared for Cynthia. Neither had Kirsten. "People aren't always what they seem. Cynthia puts up a good front. She plays the lady of the manor role to the hilt, but she knows what it's like to be poor. Before she married Jack, she scraped along on a secretary's wages. The woman has a streak of stinginess a mile wide. She resented every cent Jack spent on Kirsten, thought he favored her unfairly over Kevin. Could be all the money he dropped on the damned wedding was the final straw."

"*Damned* wedding?" She raised an eyebrow. "You weren't in favor of it?"

"Truthfully?" He grunted. "I was dead set against it. Hell, we were already married. What was the point?"

"Kirsten didn't just manipulate her father," Shea said slowly. "She manipulated you too, didn't she?"

"Kirsten . . ." He shrugged. "Nobody said no to Kirsten."

"The elopement was *her* idea, wasn't it? Kirsten's."

He stared at the scarred wooden surface of the table. "I would have married her eventually."

"But not that way, not knowing how her father felt about it. About you. What did she say to convince you?"

Oh, hell. "She told me about the baby."

Shea shifted in her seat. He couldn't read her expression but sensed he'd thrown her a curve. "The baby," she repeated. She took a deep breath and exhaled slowly. "Now Kirsten's back—without her child. How did you explain that little discrepancy to Jack?"

"I let him think Kirsten had miscarried as a result of rough handling during the kidnapping."

"Logical." She looked at him, her face inscrutable. "I wonder what really happened to the baby."

Teague knew, but he didn't enlighten her. Some secrets were best left buried.

This was a major tactical error, Shea thought. She and Teague stood side by side in the narrow Pullman kitchen, Shea washing the dishes and Teague drying them. Kirsten, Jack, murder, possession, even the puzzle of the missing baby seemed unimportant at the moment. All she could think of was Teague.

Shea was aware of his every movement, from the surprisingly deft way he handled the old white stoneware, his big hands as sure and confident as they had been on the tiller of the boat, to the casual way he leaned against the counter, waiting for her to pass him the next item to dry.

His hair was short, but the way it hugged his head suggested it would curl if allowed to grow longer. At this hour stubble darkened his jaw, giving him a rakish air.

Shea still thought he looked more like a carnival roustabout than a landscape architect.

"You don't smile enough," she said, immediately wishing she'd had the sense to keep her thoughts to herself.

Teague shot her a measuring look. "Kirsten used to tell me the same thing."

Kirsten. Always Kirsten. She let the water out of the sink, then moved past him to wipe off the counters. "I'm not Kirsten," she said evenly, not looking at him.

"Yeah, I know." He took the dishcloth from her and hung it on a rack under the sink. "Kirsten wouldn't have agreed to do the dishes. She wouldn't have known how."

Shea shrugged. "I didn't grow up with live-in servants." She glanced at her watch. "It's getting late. I should be going." When she started to move toward the living area of the big open room, he stopped her with a hand laid gently on her shoulder. "What?" she asked, turning toward him.

"Don't go. Not yet." He was totally focused on her, his intention clear.

A kiss. Oh, yes. She'd been waiting for this since that moment on the dock.

Teague bent his head to press his lips to hers with a gentle pressure. Too gentle. Too controlled. It drove her crazy.

She stood on tiptoe, straining toward him, but he pulled back, never quite breaking contact while deftly, wickedly, resisting all her efforts to deepen the kiss.

Frustration honed her need; heat built in waves. Her body buzzed and tingled in places far removed from her lips. And even farther removed from his. "Please," she whispered. "Kiss me right."

"Tell me what you want," he said, his voice rough with passion.

So she told him. She wrapped her arms around his neck, pressed herself hard against him, and pulled his face down to hers, telling him with actions instead of words, deepening the kiss and demanding the fulfillment of the fantasy she'd been toying with on and off all evening.

He tasted of coffee, warm and rich and sweet.

Shea broke away at last, breathing hard, her pulse pounding, and rested her flushed face against his chest, where his heart beat a fast, steady rhythm. She felt flustered and a little embarrassed at having so thoroughly lost herself in the moment. Apparently food wasn't the only thing she had an appetite for.

He touched her cheek fleetingly, then, grasping her chin, turned her face up toward his.

She licked her lips and smiled lazily. "Your chin feels like sandpaper," she said. "Must be a full moon."

"What?" His muscles went rigid beneath her hands. His expression tautened with suspicion. "*What* did you say?"

Shea raised an eyebrow at the harshness of his tone. "Just that your chin was scratchy. It's no big deal, nothing to get in a huff over. The truth is, stubble looks a lot sexier than it feels."

"No," he said. "The exact words. What were your exact words?" He held her close, but it wasn't a lover's embrace.

Shea was confused and a little nervous. What was going on? What had she said to spark such an emotional reaction? She searched her memory, but her exact words eluded her. "I don't know. I can't remember."

Teague's face frightened her. The remnants of arousal were mixed with some darker emotion she neither recognized nor understood. At that moment, he seemed capable of anything.

" 'Must be a full moon.' " His voice was raw, as if his words bled from a mortal wound. "That's how Kirsten explained my stubble. She used to joke that I was descended from a long line of werewolves."

Shea stiffened. She drew a deep breath, but it didn't help. "Damn you, Teague Harris. Damn you. I am *not* Kirsten. It was a stupid coincidence. That's all."

Her eyes filled with tears of anger and frustration. Why did he have so much trouble accepting the fact that she wasn't Kirsten? *Because, you fool, Kirsten's the one he wants.*

"I'm sorry, Shea. Don't cry."

She jerked away from him. "I'm mad, dammit, and I'll cry if I want to." Like that old Lesley Gore record of her mother's, she thought, and nearly choked on a sudden spurt of involuntary laughter.

God, she must be hysterical, laughing and crying at the same time.

"I'm sorry," Teague said again, the way men always do when women start crying and they don't exactly know why but figure it can't hurt to apologize.

Me too, she thought, disappointment a bitter taste at the back of her throat.

FOUR

Shea staggered down the attic stairs, balancing a stack of heavy photo albums, her third load—in case anyone was counting—and her last, thank goodness. Her poor arms felt as if they were about to rip loose from their sockets, and she was heartily sorry she'd ever fallen in with Cynthia's suggestion that she look through family photographs "to fill in the gaps in her memory."

"Watch out for that bottom step, Miss Kirsten," Glory warned. "Tread's got a wiggle in it."

"I remember," Shea said. How could she forget after the header she'd taken on her first trip down?

Despite the fact that she was hefting a load every bit as awkward and heavy as Shea's, Glory set a killing pace along the second-story hall.

"Slow down!" Shea begged, panting like the star pupil in a Lamaze class.

"Sorry." Smiling sheepishly, Glory paused outside Kirsten's bedroom door and waited for Shea to catch up.

As Shea drew even with the girl, she became aware of a low hum. "What's that?"

"What's what?"

"The humming sound. Can't you hear it?"

"I don't hear anything." Glory's face was empty of expression. Too empty.

"It's coming from my old room, I think." Shea set her load down on the floor and pressed her ear to the door. The humming stopped. "Could someone be inside? Maybe your mother is vacuuming."

"I was in there first thing this morning, washing the dormer windows," Glory admitted cautiously, "but nobody's inside now. Couldn't be. I locked up afterward. The key's in my pocket."

"Maybe you left something on. The stereo or a radio."

"Didn't turn anything on. Not even the lights." She cocked her head to listen. "I don't know what you're talking about, Miss Kirsten. I can't hear a thing."

The humming resumed as abruptly as it had stopped, a little louder this time. "There!" Shea said. "Don't tell me you can't hear that."

Glory shrugged, and the top album slid off her pile to land with a thump on the floor.

Shea started to lean over to pick it up, then froze as a second noise drowned out the low hum, a piteous whine followed by whimpering sobs. She straightened with a jerk. "My God! I suppose you didn't hear that, either."

Glory's face was pasty. "Sounds like a baby," she whispered.

A baby? Or the ghost of a baby? Shea tensed, listening intently.

The whimpers escalated to an eldritch howling accompanied by a series of loud thumps and frantic scratching noises. "No," she said, relieved. "It sounds like a dog."

A door farther along the hall banged open and Kevin Rainey strode out wearing nothing but a worried expression and a pair of blue silk boxers. "What on earth is that ungodly noise?"

"I think Beelzebub got locked inside"—Kirsten's room, Shea almost said but caught herself in time—"my room."

Glory's chagrin was painful to see. "He must have sneaked in behind my back when I was washing windows."

Another tremendous thump shook the door. Beelzebub howled like a tormented lost soul.

Kevin frowned. "I don't get it. You're back, Kirsten. So why's your room still locked?"

"Been locked for seven years. Mr. Jack's orders. Mama says until he tells us otherwise . . ." Glory stared at the floor.

The dog howled.

"Jeez, poor old Bub sounds like he's in pain. Which he will be, if we don't get him out of there before Ruth comes up to check out the racket. Where's the key?"

Glory dug a key ring from her pocket and passed it to Kevin. "I'm sorry," she said. "This is all my fault." She sounded as if she was on the verge of tears.

Kevin patted her shoulder. "Don't sweat it, Glo. It's not that big a deal."

"No, but you know what Mama's like."

"Yeah, unfortunately, I do." He opened the door, releasing the frantic dog, who headed toward the stairs at top speed, spinning his wheels on the slippery wooden floor.

"W-wait!" Glory stammered as he started to close the door. "Bub likes to hide under Miss Kirsten's bed."

"Gotcha." Kevin nodded. "And you're afraid he left one of his treasures behind."

"It's the thing Mama hates most about him. He left a dead bird under the dining-room table yesterday." She shuddered. "Before you lock up, let me check for hidden treasure."

"Go for it." He stood aside.

Glory scuttled around him, knelt by the bed, and peeked beneath the bedskirt. "Ugh!" She backed away with a shudder.

"What?" Kevin demanded.

"Dead snake?" Shea guessed, gauging the degree of the girl's revulsion.

"No." Glory shuddered again. "It's a b-bone. A b-big bone."

Kevin gave her arm a squeeze. "I'll dispose of it if you lock up." He flipped Glory the keys. "Bones don't bother me." He retrieved the macabre object and took off toward the stairs, moving almost as quickly as the dog had.

Glory stared after him.

"There's one mystery solved," Shea said.

"Mystery?" Glory asked.

"The noise. You know, you almost had me convinced I was imagining it." Shea picked up her stack of photo albums, straightening just in time to catch an unguarded expression on Glory's face. The girl looked uneasy, almost scared. And no wonder, the way her mother overreacted to every minor peccadillo. "It was an accident, the dog getting locked in that way," Shea reassured her. "Could have happened to anyone. I won't tell your mother, and I know Kevin won't, either."

Shea had been holed up in the family room looking through photos for over two hours when Kevin strolled in. "Having fun?" he asked. His grin was infectious.

Shea grinned back. "A thrill a minute."

He flopped down on the sofa, kicking a couple of needlepoint pillows aside to accommodate his feet.

"You're going to get the furniture dirty." The treads of his size-thirteen running shoes were full of mud.

"That's why we pay Ruth an exorbitant salary." He leaned back against the sofa cushions, lacing his hands behind his head. A slight smile curved his mouth as he studied her. "Tell me, when are you planning to move back in with Teague?"

She arched an eyebrow and gazed at him in silence for a full ten-count. "Why? Do you have money riding on it?"

Surprise flickered across his face, followed by reluctant admiration. "As a matter of fact, I do. They're placing bets down at the club. Almost three thousand bucks in the pot. Can't blame me for trying to get some inside info, can you?"

"If I were you, I'd save my money. No guarantees Teague and I will ever get back together."

He looked up with a devilish grin. "Don't give me that. I saw the way he looks at you."

How *does* he look at me? she wanted to ask.

Instead she passed him a snapshot. "Any idea who these people are?"

Kevin took the photograph but instead of examining it, stared fixedly at her left hand.

"What?" she asked.

"Where's your ring?"

"My ring?"

"Your engagement ring." He captured her bare left hand. "That huge square-cut aquamarine surrounded by diamonds and set in platinum. You never took it off, not even after the knock-down, drag-out you and Teague had. Don't tell me the kidnappers stole it."

The back of her neck prickled. She shrugged, feigning unconcern. "They must have." She tugged her hand free and tapped the photograph. It showed a man and two women standing next to a palm tree in front of a big stucco building. "Recognize these people?"

Kevin shrugged. "The guy's Dad and I think the woman on the right is Elizabeth, his first wife. Your mother," he added, giving her a look she couldn't quite interpret. "But I don't recognize the blonde in the middle."

Cynthia came in with another armload of albums. "I found these stuck in one of the bookcases in Jack's room," she said.

"Hey, Mom, do you know who this is?" Kevin held the photo of Jack, Elizabeth, and the mystery woman out to Cynthia.

"No feet on the furniture," she said automatically as she took the picture. "How did you get so muddy just running across to the post office?"

"I have an affinity for dirt," he said with an impudent grin, but he did sit up and prop his feet on the coffee table.

Cynthia frowned. "Brat."

"But you're crazy about me, huh? Admit it. I'm your favorite."

Cynthia fought to maintain a stern demeanor, but the corners of her mouth twitched. "I doubt Ruth shares my weakness. Go change your shoes before she throws a tantrum."

Kevin stood with exaggerated courtesy, then swept a courtly bow made only slightly ludicrous by his shorts and polo shirt. When a guy looked like Prince Charming, he could get away with a lot. "Okay, Mommy dearest. Help Kirsten identify the people in that picture, will you?"

He left, and Cynthia took his place on the sofa. "This is Jack and Elizabeth. I don't know who the other woman is, but judging by the clothing and hairstyles, I'd say the snapshot was taken in the early seventies. And not around here. California maybe?" She frowned. "The odd part is, I don't believe I've ever seen this picture before. In fact, I've never seen this album before. Must be one of your mother's. Where did you find it?" Cynthia turned to her with a questioning look.

"The attic."

Cynthia nodded, then shrugged. "Well, I'm sorry I can't be any more help. Jack might know. You could ask him."

Shea shook her head. "It's not important," she lied. The truth was, she recognized the blonde. She'd know her mother anywhere—even wearing sunglasses, bellbottoms, and hair to her waist.

"Are you ready for a break?" Cynthia asked. "Your father'd like to talk to you."

Jack Rainey seemed a little more alert than he had the day before. He greeted Shea with a smile as she leaned down to kiss his cheek. "Hi, Daddy."

"Hi yourself, baby. Cynthia said you've been looking through old photographs. Did anything trigger your memory?" He waved her toward a chair by the bed.

She sat, crossing and uncrossing her legs, fidgeting with her shirttail. "Not my memory, no. Just my curiosity." She passed him the photograph of her mother standing between him and his wife. "Who's the woman in the middle? Neither Kevin nor Cynthia recognized her."

Jack's expression stilled for a moment, but he recovered quickly. "Nobody special," he said. "One of your mother's friends. I don't recall her name."

Nobody special? I don't recall her name? Liar, she thought, bitterness like a sour taste in her mouth.

"Is something wrong?"

Despite his illness, Jack Rainey's mental faculties were sharp. She forced a smile. "Nothing," she said, proving that she could lie as well as he.

"Has Cynthia talked to you yet about moving back home?"

She nodded. "She brought it up, but . . ." She shrugged. "Daddy, I've been Shea McKenzie for so long. Yes, the memories of my old life are coming back, but I'm still more Shea than Kirsten. I need time to adjust, Daddy. Time and space."

"But if you were here, back in your old room—"

Mikey burst into the room. "Daddy, Beelzebub's missing!"

No wonder, thought Shea. He was probably holed up somewhere recovering from this morning's trauma.

"When did you see him last?" Jack asked.

"Not since last night." Mikey's face puckered up.

Shea cleared her throat. "He was around earlier this morning. I saw him." She didn't go into detail. No need to get Glory in trouble.

"Kevin did too." Mikey nodded. "But when I whistled for Bub a few minutes ago, he didn't come. And he *always* comes."

"He probably just didn't hear you," Shea said.

Mikey shot her a withering look. "He *always* comes," she repeated. She turned back to her father. "What if he tangled with another porcupine? Remember last time, Daddy? He had quills in his mouth and both front feet."

"Not a discriminating pugilist," Jack agreed with a faint smile.

The young girl frowned. "I'm worried. I tried to get Kevin to help me look for him, but he would rather play stupid old tennis with his stupid old friends than help me find my dog. And Mom won't let me search alone. She says it's not safe." Mikey's expression explained very clearly what she thought of such excessive adult concern. Shea suspected Jack and Cynthia tended to be a little overprotective since Kirsten's kidnapping.

"Maybe Hal and Glory could help," Jack suggested.

Mikey's sour expression spoke volumes. "They're both busy doing God's work. That's what Ruth says. Only it looks like licking envelopes to me."

"Then I guess you'll have to wait until Kevin gets back," her father said.

Mikey's chin quivered. "He's staying in Liberty late to go to some dumb party at the club. By the time he gets back, Beelzebub could be dead."

"I don't know what else to suggest." Jack's bony fingers clenched at the top edge of the sheet.

"I'll help you look for your dog," Shea offered, more affected by the helplessness on Jack Rainey's face than she cared to admit.

Mikey shot her a startled glance, apparently having forgotten until then that Shea was there. "All right," she said grudgingly, as if she were the one doing Shea a favor.

Teague had assumed Shea was on the island, but his heart still gave a lurch when he spotted her and Mikey walking across the clearing toward the gazebo.

"You sure you want me to cut down this tree, boss?" His foreman tapped the base of a big pine. "It falls wrong, and it's gonna take out half the gazebo."

Teague grinned. "Then you damned well better see it falls right."

The sound of the chain saw drowned out Nick's grumbling.

Teague walked over to meet Shea and Mikey. "What brings you ladies up here?"

"We're looking for Beelzebub," Mikey said. "Have you seen him?"

Teague knelt on one knee so that he could look the little girl in the eye. "He hasn't been around. What's going on? He playing hide-and-seek?"

"Something like that," Shea said. "We've been all over the island searching for him, but we can't find him anywhere. We were hoping maybe he'd heard your crew making noise and come up here to investigate."

"Sorry. I haven't seen hide nor hair of him." He

stood. "You ladies look hot and tired, though. Why don't you take a break? We've got drinks in the cooler back behind the gazebo if you're thirsty."

"Thanks," Shea said. "I think we've covered this island from one end to the other, anyway. We've just about run out of places to search."

Mikey looked glum. "Somebody must have kidnapped him."

"I doubt it, kiddo, but maybe he did stow away on someone's boat without their realizing it. Anybody make any trips to town this morning?"

"Kevin went to the post office," Shea said.

"Hal went across to pick up groceries and stuff like he always does on Mondays." Mikey frowned. "Then later Kevin went to the club."

"And my men have been back and forth a couple of times, hauling in equipment."

"So I guess he could have sneaked a ride." Shea looked doubtful. The dog was big as a horse and friendly as a horse thief, not the sort of animal it would be easy to overlook.

"Maybe." Mikey didn't look convinced, either. Suddenly she froze. "Did you hear that?"

Something was crashing toward them through the underbrush.

"Beelzebub?" Mikey's face brightened, then fell as Hallelujah Griffin stumbled into the clearing, loaded down with fishing gear.

He blinked at them in surprise. The boy was at the awkward, gangly stage, with knobby knees and big-knuckled hands.

"Hey, I thought you were busy with God's work," Mikey accused.

He shuffled his feet and smiled sheepishly. "My tongue got sore from licking all them flaps, so I told Mama I had chores to finish up in the garden plot."

"Going to stake tomatoes with that fishing pole, are you?" Teague asked, and the boy blushed.

"You shouldn't lie to your mother," Mikey told him sternly.

"She shouldn't volunteer me to work on the reverend's newsletter. Like anybody reads that stuff, anyway." He looked a little uneasy, as if he were afraid God—or the Reverend Dwayne Culpepper—was about to smite him for blasphemy. He remained unsmitten, however.

"Have you seen Beelzebub?" Mikey asked.

"Nope," Hal said, "but I'll keep an eye peeled."

Mikey watched him head for the shoreline and out of sight, her face a study in dejection.

"How long have you two been searching?" Teague asked Shea.

She shrugged. "I don't know. A couple hours, I guess."

"Two hours is a long time," he said. "I bet Beelzebub's home waiting for you, Mikey."

Her face lit up. "You really think so?"

Teague tugged gently at her ponytail. "No way to tell for sure, but it's worth checking out, isn't it, shortcake? Tell you what. I'll get you ladies something to drink, then walk back down to the house with you. I've got a couple of job-related questions for Jack, anyway."

Shea placed a hand on Teague's arm as the path emerged into the meadow above the cabin. "Watch Mikey," she said.

The little girl lay down at the top of the slope, criss-crossed her arms over her chest as if she was hugging herself, then rolled like a barrel down the grassy incline.

Teague turned to her in surprise. "You knew she was going to do that?"

Shea laughed. "I guessed. It's what I used to do. Got in big trouble too, for getting grass stains all over my clothes. Ruth had a thing about grass stains."

Teague gave her a funny look.

Her smile faded as she realized what she'd said. "Oh, boy. I did it again, huh?" Spoken from Kirsten's point of view. The slip frightened her.

"There must be a rational explanation," he said.

She cocked her head. "Yeah? Like what? I've suddenly developed full-blown schizophrenia? Only instead of hearing voices, I think other people's thoughts?"

"Is that any crazier than your explanation? I'm supposed to believe Kirsten's ghost is trying to possess your body?"

Shea turned toward the lake. The surface was glassy in the sheltering curve of the island, but farther out whitecaps danced. "Believe what you want."

"Shea?" Teague put his arms around her and turned her to face him. "I'm sorry if you thought I was calling you a liar. But . . ."

"I know," she said. "I wouldn't believe it, either, if it were happening to someone else."

He kissed the tip of his finger and pressed it to her lips. "You must hate me for involving you in this mess."

"Hate you? No." *Not hardly. In fact, I think I'm falling in love with you. Which is pretty damn depressing since it's obvious you're still hung up on your missing wife.* She sighed.

"Did you know they're laying bets at the country club on how long it'll be before I move in with you?"

Teague was fifteen minutes early. He and Shea had arranged to meet at the dock by the boathouse for the trip to Massacre Island. Cynthia had invited them to dinner.

Hearing a noise, he glanced up. His heart skipped a beat when he saw Shea sauntering down the dock toward him like a model on a Paris runway. She looked gorgeous—slim, tanned, vital—her silky dark hair swirling around her shoulders, her mouth curved in a sexy smile, her eyes hidden by a pair of oversize sunglasses. She wore a slinky little sundress, very short, formfitting on top with a flared skirt. Aquamarine, Kirsten's signature color.

"Ready?" she called.

"Where did you get that dress?" He almost choked on his words.

Her footsteps faltered. "Why? Don't you like it?"

"Whether or not I like it isn't the issue. Where did you get it?"

She eyed him warily. "I didn't have anything suitable, so Cynthia loaned me this little number. Is there a problem?"

"That dress isn't Cynthia's."

One eyebrow arched above her sunglasses. "I get it. You're irritated because she loaned me something of Kirsten's. Lighten up. As far as Cynthia knows, I *am* Kirsten."

"It's just . . ." He helped her into the boat. She took a seat in the bow, tugging at the abbreviated skirt. "It's just that it brings back memories. Kirsten was wearing that dress the last time I saw her." When they'd fought so bitterly. Not one of his all-time favorite memories.

"This dress?" Shea looked surprised. "She must not have been very far along."

He cast off. Edging past her, he made his way to the tiller. "I don't follow."

"In her pregnancy." She grinned, revealing that elusive dimple, and his blood pressure made a quantum leap up the scale. "This dress doesn't leave much to the imagination."

Teague grinned back. The scope of his imagination might surprise her.

Mikey, flanked by Glory and Hal, was waiting for them on the dock. The little girl was resplendent in a pink sundress and matching hair ribbon. "We've been waiting for hours," she complained.

"Ten minutes," corrected the literal-minded Glory.

"Mikey's a little antsy," Hal told them.

"I am not," she said with dignity. "I had a bath."

"Catch anything?" Teague asked Hal as he helped Shea onto the dock.

A mistake.

The boy blushed and stammered an incoherent reply.

His sister rounded on him immediately. "Were you *fishing*, Hal Griffin?" Her voice rose. "I thought you told Mama you had to work in the garden!" Glory harangued her poor brother all the way across the island. Why should he get to goof off when she was stuck with the Reverend Dwayne Culpepper's fifteen hundred newsletters-slash-solicitations?

"Don't tell Mama," he pleaded, his voice cracking.

"We wouldn't think of it," Shea said. "Would we, Teague?" Her glance was a reproof.

He felt like a jerk. "Did Beelzebub ever show up?" he asked in an effort to turn the conversation in a safer direction.

Unfortunately, the reminder plunged Mikey into gloom. "No. I think he's been dognapped."

But after such an inauspicious start, the evening went surprisingly well. Jack joined them for dinner, which made it a festive occasion. Mikey's centerpiece of driftwood and wildflowers drew oohs and ahs, and Ruth Griffin had done herself proud, serving stuffed lake trout, baked potatoes with sour cream and chives, fresh steamed vegetables from the garden, and melt-in-the-mouth huckleberry muffins.

The only uncomfortable moment came just as Ruth brought out dessert. Teague was watching for Shea's reaction to the flaky apple turnovers when Jack announced, "I'm changing my will to include Kirsten," so he saw the way her expression congealed.

Someone sucked in his or her breath in a hiss.

Teague glanced up in time to catch the poisonous look the housekeeper shot in Shea's direction. Then he surveyed the others' reactions. Cynthia appeared momentarily startled before her face relaxed in a smile, but Mikey wasn't as accomplished a dissembler as her mother. Her mouth tightened and she mumbled something about "nimposters" under her breath.

Shea didn't say a word, just stared at the floor as if she wished it would open up and swallow her whole.

"Isn't anyone going to say anything?" Jack demanded.

"I think that's very nice, dear," Cynthia said with a

charming smile for Shea, though since Shea was still staring at the floor, she missed it.

"Well, what I think is—" Mikey broke off abruptly, as
if her mother had kicked her under the table.

Shea managed a smile for Jack, but Teague noticed
that she left her dessert untouched.

FIVE

The evening was cool with just enough breeze off the water to keep the mosquitoes at bay. Very aware of her hand, small and warm in his, Teague led Shea down the path to the beach. After dinner, Cynthia had suggested that Teague take Shea for a walk. "You never know what might release a new flood of memories."

Shea had shot him a look, as if to say, "I have quite enough memories of my own, thank you very much," but once outside, she'd seemed to relax.

Across the lake the lights of Liberty formed a bright semicircle of sparkling pinpricks in the gathering darkness. A spectacular sunset reflected orange, red, pink, and lavender in shimmering ripples on the surface of the water. The surrounding mountains loomed black and featureless by contrast.

They walked hand in hand, neither of them inclined to talk. Tiny wavelets lapped onto the sandy beach. The scent of pine mingled with the more delicate fragrance of the sweet peas that grew wild along the ledges.

Shea tugged him to a halt near the water's edge. "Wait a sec. I want to slip off my shoes." She laughed, a soft, low sound that sent prickles of awareness down his spine. "I can't remember the last time I went barefoot in the sand."

To keep himself from latching on to her and kissing her senseless, Teague chose a flat stone from the pebbles littering the beach and sent it skipping across the water. "Shea?"

"What?" She smiled up at him, her face gilded by the warm glow of the setting sun.

I'm crazy about you. I love the way you walk, the way you talk, the way you laugh . . . the way you eat, for crying out loud. "Nothing." He sent another stone spinning off into the darkness.

Unaware of his inner turmoil, she stared at the jagged skyline. "You've known Jack a long time, right?"

"Long enough. Why?"

"How would you characterize him?" Her voice was a shade too casual.

"What are you getting at?"

She shrugged. "Like you said before, the resemblance between Kirsten and me can't be a coincidence." She paused, sighing heavily. "My mother told me that my real father died in Vietnam, but what if he didn't die? What if . . ." Her words trailed off into a troubled silence.

"You suspect your mother had an affair with Jack?"

"The possibility has crossed my mind." She sighed again.

"But, Shea, according to your driver's license, you were born on July fifteenth. Kirsten was born on June fifth of the same year. So that means Jack would have to have been sleeping with both your mother and his wife at the same time." He narrowed his gaze. "No way. I'd place the odds that Jack Rainey cheated on his wife at a million to one. It's not his style."

"But—"

"What's a helluva lot more likely is that your father was related to Jack. Brother, cousin, something like that. Hell, maybe Jack has a black-sheep twin brother nobody talks about. Ask him to fill you in on family history."

Shea balled her hands into fists. "Maybe I'll do that."

Capturing her right hand in his, he said, "In the meantime, though, don't tie yourself in knots over it. Didn't anyone ever tell you stress is bad for your health?" He stroked the soft skin of her palm with slow, languid movements, then gently massaged the tension from her fingers one by one—a really dumb move on his part as far as reducing his own stress level was concerned. Before, he'd been obsessed with touching her. Now that he *was* touching her, all he could think about was how much he wanted to kiss her. Kiss her and . . .

Her hand trembled in his.

Oh, hell. Stress be damned. Teague pulled her into his arms.

Shea pressed a hand to his chest. He thought for a second she was going to shove him away, but she didn't. Instead she cupped his chin with her free hand, trailing her fingers across his jaw in a tender caress.

He sucked in a ragged breath, wondering if she felt the sudden acceleration of his heartbeat.

She slid her hand up to curve around the back of his neck, leaning into him, soft and yielding. Her hair flowed across her shoulders in silken waves. She smelled faintly of coconut. "Kiss me," she said.

"Pretty bossy, aren't you?"

"Occupational hazard. Executives get used to giving orders." She rubbed against his body with an agonizing friction. She was soft and warm, and he wanted her. The question was, did she want him?

"Shea?"

"Kiss me," she whispered, and, dragging his mouth down to meet hers, took him, body and soul. An outsider would only have seen a kiss, but Teague knew better. She branded him hers with the searing touch of her lips, sealing his fate with the stroke of her tongue.

This is crazy, he thought. For all he knew, she could be a con woman after the Rainey fortune. But at the moment he didn't care. Nothing mattered except the hot, sweet taste of her on his tongue, the heavy warmth of her lush curves filling his hands.

"It's been so long," he whispered, and felt her stiffen.

She jerked away. "Kirsten," she said. "You thought I was Kirsten, didn't you?"

"No, I—"

"You said 'It's been so long.'"

"I meant it's been so long since I felt this way about anyone. Dammit, I think I'm falling in love with you, Shea."

She studied his face in the fading light, a look of infinite sadness shadowing her eyes. "I wish I could believe that."

"Believe it."

Sighing, she slipped her shoes back on. "Let's walk a little farther. I need to clear my head."

So did he. *Had* he confused her with Kirsten? He didn't think so, but he wasn't one hundred percent sure. Shea evoked the same heady mixture of emotions, the same overwhelming desire. He couldn't think straight when he was touching her, couldn't think at all when he was kissing her.

They followed the shore for a hundred yards or more in silence. Teague was half afraid to say anything for fear of putting his foot in his mouth again.

Shea was the first to break the uncomfortable silence. "I'm curious about something."

"What?"

"You really seem to care about Jack Rainey, but I don't understand why. Seven years ago the man did everything in his power to turn his daughter against you. Yet now you're friends. What happened? When did things change?"

"When Kirsten was kidnapped, Jack and I discovered we had a lot in common." *Guilt*, he thought, but didn't say. "I had a hard time dealing with her sudden disappearance. I blamed everyone—Kirsten, Jack, and, most of all, myself. I drank, hoping to forget."

Her eyes looked huge. "You must have loved her . . . Kirsten . . . very much."

Teague kicked a piece of driftwood out of his path. "Yes, I did." Right up until the day of the fight. "But that's no excuse for my behavior. I was out of control. Self-destructive." He stopped. He wasn't proud of that chapter of his life. He didn't like thinking about it, let alone talking about it.

"We all handle grief in different ways," she said softly.

Teague met her gaze. "But some ways are a hell of a lot more effective than others." He laughed sourly. "One night I picked a fight with the wrong guy and got myself busted up pretty bad, got tossed in the drunk tank with a couple of winos. Jack bailed me out." A faint smile tilted the corners of his mouth at the memory, though it hadn't been very funny at the time. "He cussed me up one side and down the other, asked me was this the kind of man Kirsten would want to come home to?"

"So you straightened up?"

"Not right away, but that was the beginning. I don't have any family. I figured nobody gave a rip what happened to me. Only, for some reason, Jack did. He kept after me to clean up my act, and eventually I did. I went back to school, earned a degree, started the landscaping business."

"I see." She glanced back toward the house. "You owe him."

"Big time." He nodded. "If Jack Rainey hadn't pestered the bejeezers out of me, by now I'd probably be dead or rotting in prison."

Shea examined his face carefully. "Kirsten's been gone a long time. Haven't you ever . . . I mean, is there anyone . . ."

"Anyone I'm interested in? Another woman, you mean? No," he said. *Not until you walked into my life.* "How about you? Do you have someone special you care about, Shea?"

She lowered her lashes, hiding her eyes. "I dated a man last winter. A colleague. We had a lot in common, and for a while I thought it might lead somewhere, but . . ."

"But what?"

"He asked me to marry him."

Teague tensed.

"I turned him down."

"If you were so compatible, why?"

"No fireworks. Not even sparks." She gave a gurgle of laughter, a deep throaty sound that sent a lightning bolt of desire zapping straight to his groin. "Pretty dumb, huh? Jason was rich, handsome, intelligent—in short, Mr. Perfect, and I turned him down because he didn't give me goose bumps."

"Shea?"

"Hmm?" She turned to face him, her hair swirling around her shoulders in a dark cloud.

He brushed a strand away from her cheek. "Do *I* give you goose bumps?"

She shivered slightly and shifted her gaze away from his. "I don't know if it's you or just the breeze off the lake. Maybe we should get moving."

Teague didn't argue. If she wasn't ready, there was no point in pushing it.

They climbed a tumble of giant boulders, untidy debris left behind by the glacier that had gouged out Crescent Lake. The rocks formed an arm that jutted out into the lake to enclose the cove. "Watch your step," Teague said, taking her arm.

The wind was stronger on the point than it had been in the protection of the cove. Shivering, Shea snuggled into his embrace.

The rocks of the point gave way to another, smaller cove, a tiny silvery arc of sand hemmed in by trees, huge old timbers that probably had been fully grown when Lewis and Clark first explored this part of the country.

Just beyond the cove on a rugged stretch of shoreline, where the trees yielded to slanting granite ledges, Shea felt the first tendrils of panic wrap themselves around her heart. "Did you hear something?" she asked Teague, surprised at how shaky she sounded.

"No." He gave her a sharp look. "What's wrong?"

"Nothing, I guess." She forced herself to proceed, though every instinct urged retreat. But as they approached the crevice, where a spring had cut a narrow channel through the rock, the nameless dread increased exponentially. She balked at the edge of the cleft, too terrified to move.

Teague glanced back at her. "Coming?"

She shook her head, gazing at him wide-eyed. "I can't."

"There's nothing to be afraid of. Just step across. Here, let me help you." Teague reached for her hand.

"No!" Shea backed away from the edge.

"Hey, it's only about three feet deep. There's no danger, Shea. Honest."

She shook her head again. "I'm not worried about the crevice." The source of her dread lay hidden on the other side of the stream, where the ledge dwindled to earth and the alders crowded claustrophobically close.

"Then what's the problem?" He backtracked to where she stood.

"There's something over there." She pointed to the deep shadows behind him. "Something or someone. I can feel it."

He inclined his head, as if he were listening. The silence was complete. "Probably just a porcupine."

"Maybe," she said, not believing it for a second.

Nearby, a twig broke with a sharp crack. The underbrush rustled a furtive warning.

Teague stiffened. "Beelzebub? Is that you, boy?"

More twigs snapped, even closer this time. Shea felt

as if a hundred hostile eyes were glaring at them from the shadows. "I don't like this, Teague. Let's go back," she whispered. "Please."

"I doubt it's anything more sinister than a raccoon."

"Please?"

His gaze held hers for an endless moment. Then he shrugged. "All right."

Shea didn't talk much on the trip back across the lake to Strawberry Point. She kept remembering the irrational fear she'd felt at the edge of the alder thicket. Had the danger been real? she wondered. Or another of Kirsten's memories?

Teague glanced at his watch. "It's early yet. Why don't you come in for a cup of coffee?"

"I'm tired." And confused. If she agreed to visit his apartment, that was like admitting she was interested in him. And okay, she *was* interested, but the problem was, she wasn't sure who he was interested in—Shea McKenzie or Kirsten Rainey.

Teague pulled her into his arms, looking down into her face with such a tender, loving expression, she felt as if her heart were about to batter its way past her rib cage. "You don't look tired to me. Please stay. Just for a few minutes."

Don't do it, warned her better judgment, but her better judgment couldn't feel the warmth of his embrace or see the smoky promise in his eyes.

"Okay," she agreed. "Just for a few minutes."

He dropped a quick kiss on her forehead.

All of a sudden Shea's legs felt wobbly. She was thankful for the support of his arm around her waist as he led her up the steep outside staircase. She leaned against the railing, gulping air, while he fought with the lock.

The tumblers clicked at last and he shouldered the door open, pulling her inside. "Hit the lights, would you?"

Shea fumbled along the wall until she found the switch. She flipped it, then gasped in surprise at the chaotic scene that met her eyes.

Teague swore nonstop for a full minute. "Sorry," he apologized once he had himself under control.

"No problem." She glanced around the room. "Either you're the world's messiest housekeeper or you've had a visit from the trash fairy."

The room was a disaster. It looked as if a tornado had touched down inside, overturning furniture, ripping out drawers, and tumbling bookcases. The sugar and flour canisters spilled their contents over the counter and onto the floor, where they mingled with cornflakes and pasta. Some of the residue had been tracked across the wooden floor and ground into the colorful Chinese rug that defined the living area.

"What the hell were they looking for?" he demanded, surveying the ruin in disgust.

"Good question. Did you have any large sums of money on the premises?"

"No, though I see the TV and VCR are missing."

"Yeah, but why pull out the drawers and dump the canisters if all they were after was electronic equipment? They must have been searching for something else."

He shrugged his shoulders in a curiously helpless gesture. "But what? Drugs? Jewelry? A cache of guns? Who knows? All I can say for sure is that they didn't find anything worth spit. I keep my valuables in a safe-deposit box."

Shea froze as another possibility occurred to her. "Could this be connected somehow with Kirsten?"

"What? You think a ghost trashed my apartment?"

"No, but maybe whoever's responsible for her disappearance did. Maybe he thinks you have some evidence implicating him in her death."

He shook his head. "Seems unlikely, but who knows? I guess we'll have a better idea who's responsible once we discover what's missing. I'd better call the sheriff's department and report this."

He grabbed a dishtowel from a pile on the floor and used it to lift the telephone receiver from its cradle. He dialed by poking the buttons with the eraser end of a pencil. After explaining the situation in a few terse sentences, he hung up.

"They're going to send someone right out to investigate," he told her, "but I need to go into town to make a report." His narrow-eyed gaze roved over the destruction, settling finally on her. "I want you to follow me to the sheriff's office in your car."

Shea shifted her weight uneasily from one foot to the other. "You don't need me. I'll just be in the way. I think I'll head back to the lodge."

"No!" he all but shouted. In a quieter tone he said, "No. If you're right about the Kirsten connection, whoever did this may have broken into your room too. They may still be there. I don't want you going anywhere alone."

His tone of voice made it clear there was no point in arguing with him. Not that Shea felt inclined to argue. The wanton destruction in his apartment made her feel sick to her stomach. The last thing she wanted right now was to be alone.

As she followed the glowing red of his taillights, her mind raced in circles. Even if someone suspected Teague had put her up to the Kirsten charade, why break into his apartment? What had they hoped to find? Proof linking the two of them? Something that showed she wasn't Kirsten? Her head was aching with a dull throb by the time she pulled into the parking lot next to the Crescent County Sheriff's Department.

She sat on a hard plastic chair opposite the main desk while Teague gave his statement. The room was chilly. She hugged herself, wishing she had worn a sweater.

What was taking Teague so long, anyway? She yawned. At this time of night, the place was virtually deserted. Since Teague and the deputy had disappeared into a warren of partitioned rooms, she'd seen only the dispatcher, a bulldog-faced woman who was glued to the switchboard. Since the first searching appraisal, the woman had steadfastly ignored her. *Probably thinks I'm a hooker in this damn dress.*

The minutes ticked slowly by. Shea shifted in her chair, trying to find a comfortable position. She yawned again. A cup of coffee might help.

"Is there a coffee machine around here?" she asked.

Either the dispatcher was ignoring her or the headset she was wearing interfered with her hearing.

Shea stood and stretched, then walked over to the desk and waited until the woman acknowledged her.

Bulldog removed her headpiece. "Yeah?"

"Is there a coffee—"

The front door burst open to admit a noisy crowd that eventually resolved itself into one harassed-looking deputy, an obstreperous drunk, a clean-cut Ivy League type, and a pale, weepy redhead who clung to Joe College like a cocklebur.

Of the four, Shea recognized only one. "Kevin?"

"Kirsten?"

"What are *you* doing here?" they asked in chorus.

"Son of a bitch blocked my Caddie, that's what!" bellowed the drunk. "Young snots think they own the whole damn world."

"We'll take your statement in a minute, Mr. Walsh," the deputy told him, then turned to Kevin. "Why don't you and Miss Ames have a seat, Mr. Rainey? I'll take your statements after Mr. Walsh has made his."

"Damn right you will," said the fuming drunk. "Ask the little punk what he was doing blocking my Caddie that way. Damn kids think they can do whatever the hell they want."

The officer, his studied courtesy severely strained, ushered the loudmouthed Mr. Walsh toward one of the partitioned cubicles.

Shea raised her eyebrows. "What's going on?"

Kevin glanced meaningfully at the dispatcher. "Let's sit down and I'll fill you in."

Shea returned to her seat, and Kevin dragged a pair of chairs from the line against the wall, turning them to face Shea.

"I don't like this, Kevin, and my parents aren't going to like it, either." The redhead looked as if she were about to burst into tears.

"Don't worry, Chelsea. It's going to be all right."

"What happened?" Shea asked.

"It was awful!" Chelsea broke into noisy sobs.

Kevin calmed her down, then turned to Shea. "What brings you here?"

"Somebody broke into Teague's apartment. We came in to report it. Now quit trying to change the subject. Tell me about your accident."

He shrugged. "Not much to tell. Old man Walsh got a snootful, then decided to play bumper cars in the parking lot at the club. He claims I was blocking him, but the truth is, he was too drunk to maneuver. It's a tight lot, and I was parked close, but he should have been able to get out without damaging anything. This probably isn't going to do my insurance premiums any good. They won't care whether it was my fault or not."

"What's the story, Kevin? Wreck your car again?" Teague had slipped up on them unnoticed.

Kevin seemed to shrink in stature as the older man's biting tone ripped away his thin veneer of sophistication; the boy suddenly looked younger than his nineteen years. He hesitated for a second or two, evidently trying to gauge Teague's mood.

"It wasn't his fault." The redhead spoke up. "Taggart Walsh bashed Kevin's Fiat in the parking lot at the club. On purpose, if you ask me." Her voice shook. "Look, is there someplace I can call my parents? It's getting late. They'll be worried."

"There's a pay phone down the hall by the restrooms," Kevin said.

"I don't have any money." She looked as if she was going to start bawling again.

Shea, Kevin, and Teague all whipped out quarters. The girl accepted Kevin's money and hurried off.

"Your father's not going to be a happy camper when

he hears what happened," Teague said. "What is this? Your third accident so far this year?"

"Yeah," Kevin agreed glumly. "And he's never gonna believe it wasn't my fault. He'll probably throw those gambling debts back in my face too."

"Gambling debts?" Shea echoed.

Kevin gave her a shamefaced look. "I got a little carried away betting on football last fall. My allowance wouldn't cover my losses, and I had to ask Dad for help. He was *not* pleased."

"To put it mildly," Teague said. He turned to Shea. "I'm finished here for the time being. Why don't I take you back to the lodge?"

"I have my own car," Shea reminded him.

"So I'll follow you. I want to make sure your room is secure."

They left Kevin at the police station feeling extremely sorry for himself.

Shea's room hadn't been ransacked; that was obvious as soon as they opened the door, but Teague spent a good ten minutes checking the locks on the doors and windows anyway before pronouncing himself satisfied.

"Thanks," she said.

"For what?"

She smiled and his heart gave a jolt. "For caring enough to make sure I was safe."

He cleared his throat. "Least I could do. I suppose I should go back to see if the deputies have discovered anything."

"Probably." She smiled again and he knew he wasn't going anywhere. Not yet.

He cleared his throat. "They're probably waiting for me."

"Uh-huh."

"They want me to inventory my stuff as soon as they finish dusting for prints. Apparently the intruder jimmied the back door. Used a crowbar."

"Not a pro then," she said.

"Kids, the cops figure."

"You don't sound convinced."

He cocked an eyebrow. "I'm a suspicious bastard by nature. Maybe I'll change my mind once I see what's missing. Speaking of which, I should get going."

"Yes, I suppose you should."

Still, he didn't move. "This isn't the way I had hoped to end the evening," he said at last.

"Why? What had you hoped to do?"

Teague pulled her into his arms and kissed her—thoroughly.

When he finally lifted his mouth from hers, he stared steadily into her face, not saying a word.

Shea blinked a time or two. "Oh," she murmured faintly.

He brushed a strand of soft dark hair back off her cheek. "See you tomorrow."

"Tomorrow?" she whispered, making it sound like a question.

He left her slumped against the wall, breathing hard and looking dazed. Dazed, but happy.

And despite the fact that he probably wasn't going to get any sleep at all, Teague whistled all the way back to Strawberry Point.

SIX

Shea didn't head immediately for Massacre Island the next morning even though she was anxious to get through the rest of the photo albums. She went first to the Liberty Public Library to see what information they had on possession. There she enlisted the aid of Emily Freitag, the local librarian. Ms. Freitag was eager to help Shea locate sources for her hypothetical psychology research paper since she herself had a strong interest in psi phenomena, having grown up in a haunted house.

As she put it, "I've always adored reading about 'ghoulies and ghosties and long-leggety beasties / And things that go bump in the night.'"

Since Ms. Freitag looked like the stereotypical librarian, prim and elderly with a salt-and-pepper bun, lavender-flowered dress, and glasses slipping halfway down her nose, her tastes surprised Shea, who'd had the woman pegged as the Danielle Steel type.

"I'm mainly interested in actual case studies of possession," Shea said.

"Hmm." Ms. Freitag adjusted her bifocals. "There was that incident with the boy in suburban Washington—the one William Blatty based *The Exorcist* on."

"Isn't that movie about a girl who's possessed by demons?"

The librarian nodded. "Right. In the book and the movie. But the actual case involved a little boy, and in my humble opinion, it sounded more like poltergeist activity than possession." She fell silent for a moment, staring fixedly at her computer monitor.

"Anything else?"

"Of course there are always the poor deluded souls who're convinced they've been possessed by Elvis or Napoleon."

"I don't think so."

Ms. Freitag frowned. "How about that little girl from Illinois," she said slowly, frowning fiercely as she dredged the details from the depths of her memory. "Funny name. Yancy? Delancey? Something like that. She was purportedly possessed by the soul of another girl who had died some years before."

"That sounds more like it," Shea said.

The older woman gave her an odd look. "More like what?"

"More like what I'm interested in," she said hastily. "Not possession by demons or celebrities but by plain ordinary people."

"Plain, ordinary *dead* people."

"Okay, dead people, but ordinary people who lived ordinary lives, not devils or demons or even historical figures. Where could I find something about the girl with the odd name?"

Ms. Freitag tapped away at the keyboard, then

printed out a list of relevant references. "Good luck," she said.

Volumes had been written on the topic of possession, much of it scientific or pseudo-scientific, and none of it describing phenomena resembling that of her own experiences. Even the story of young Lurancy Vennum, the Watseka Wonder, whose body supposedly had been inhabited for some months by the spirit of Mary Roff, a girl who'd died twelve years previously, offered little parallel.

Lurancy hadn't just inherited Mary's memories; she'd also inherited the girl's identity. Her own personality had disappeared. For the period of her possession, she had recognized her own family only as acquaintances, claiming Mary's family as her own. Shea's experiences weren't quite like that.

Still hoping to find a clue, she expanded her reading to include theories on racial memory and clairvoyance. The more she read, the more farfetched any of it seemed as an explanation for her own strange intuitions.

By eleven-thirty her head was aching and she was bored out of her skull. Somehow the exorcism of the nuns of Loudun in the 1600s just didn't seem relevant. Also, the increasingly loud complaints from her empty stomach had begun to interfere with her concentration.

After a frustrating couple of hours at the sheriff's office, Teague stopped off for an early lunch at the Liberty Lodge Coffee Shop. He was just about to order when he spotted Shea and waved her over.

"I hope your morning was more productive than

mine," she said, settling across from him with a sigh. "I'll take the special," she told the hovering waitress.

"Make that two," said Teague.

She was wearing her hair in a high ponytail, secured with a red scrunchie that matched her T-shirt. She looked about sixteen, whereas he, after a short night and a bureaucratic nightmare of a morning, felt like a senior citizen.

"Any news on your break-in?" she asked.

He frowned. "Not much. I finished the inventory. All that was taken was my TV, VCR, and CD player. Funny thing is, the cops found the stuff already—dumped in the lake near the boathouse."

"That's weird. If they were just going to dump it, why take it in the first place?"

"Good question. And why did the burglar leave such a shambles behind?"

"Maybe robbery wasn't the real motive."

"Or maybe the burglars stole something I'm not admitting to. That's what the investigating deputy suspects. He asked some very pointed questions this morning."

"What kind of questions?"

"About possible connections with known drug dealers or militias. Apparently he assumes I had a large sum of cash hidden on the premises, that I'm either dealing in drugs or illegal arms."

The waitress gave him an odd look as she set a cup of coffee in front of him.

He dropped a couple of ice cubes from his water glass into his coffee, then took a careful sip. "So how was your morning?"

"Not as depressing as yours." She grinned. "I went to

the library to research ghosts, possession, and related phenomena."

"And?"

"My experiences are different from any of the stuff I read about. I'm not sure what that means. Maybe I'm just losing it."

Lunch arrived then, big bowls of corn chowder and fresh homemade rolls. As Shea dove into her food, Teague realized with a stab of guilty pleasure that once again he was getting aroused just watching her eat. She enjoyed food on a sensuous level. And if she got this excited over soup and bread, he reflected, chocolate would probably send her orgasmic. He smiled into his coffee cup. Might be interesting to find out.

After lunch Shea bummed a ride with Teague to the island. As they neared the crest of the path, they heard the roar of a chain saw. "Doesn't sound like they've been slacking off in your absence."

"I've got a good foreman," he said. "Nick keeps everyone in line." He raised an eyebrow in a sardonic look. "Including me."

"You're going all the way to the house?" she asked, surprised when he didn't take the fork that led to the gazebo.

"Got some details to talk over with Jack."

He wasn't touching her, but Shea's skin felt hot and prickly anyway. She was very aware of his shoulder just inches from hers, aware too that he was spending more time watching her than the path. He stopped suddenly ten yards from the house.

"What's wrong?" she asked, turning to him, her heart beating out of control at his intent expression.

"Nothing." The air between them all but snapped with electricity. Teague's gaze held hers prisoner. "Have dinner with me tonight?"

An innocuous request, but she responded to the silent subtext, nearly drowning in the resulting wave of desire. Her pulses pounded; her stomach fluttered. She trembled in a response so powerful, it was almost painful.

Or was it Kirsten's reaction she felt?

"I'd like that," she said.

"Seven all right?"

"Perfect."

He shot her another of those high-voltage looks. *Complete core meltdown*, she thought muzzily. That pretty well summed up her reaction to Teague Harris, and frankly, she didn't care if it was secondhand emotion or not.

While Teague conferred with Jack, Shea leafed through the rest of the albums but found nothing to interest her.

Retrieving the album she'd set aside, she flipped to the picture of her mother with Jack and his first wife. Teague had suggested the existence of a black-sheep twin, but Shea didn't buy it. She remembered the way Jack's face had changed when she'd shown him the photograph. *Nobody special . . . I don't recall her name.*

Jack Rainey was her father. She was convinced of it. And her mother knew he was alive; the postcard proved it, which maybe explained why her mother had never wanted to travel to the western part of the United States. Too many skeletons buried in them thar hills.

The question was, did Jack know of Shea's existence? She pulled the postcard of Liberty from her purse. Obviously Elizabeth had known Christine well enough to drop her a line, and equally as obvious, her mother had known the Raineys had a daughter. *Our Kirsten continues to thrive.*

She frowned. But what was the rest of the message about? *If ever you need anything—anything at all—don't hesitate to contact us.* It wasn't the sort of message a woman sent to her husband's lover. Hadn't Elizabeth known about Jack's affair with Christine?

Shea pressed her fingertips to her forehead. The uncertainty was driving her crazy! Sighing, she sat up straight. She couldn't get the story from her mother— not until her mom and stepfather returned from Europe, anyway—but she could ask Jack Rainey, and she intended to, as soon as possible. She was sick of pretending to be someone she wasn't. Masquerading as a dead woman had seemed like a kindness at first, but in the long run, wasn't it better if she told them all the truth—that she was Jack's daughter, all right, just not the daughter they thought?

Unfortunately, when she stopped in to see Jack, he looked terrible, and she decided that today was not the time for upsetting revelations.

"I'm okay," he said in response to her concerned look. "Just tired after all the excitement yesterday." She took the hint and didn't stay long.

Feeling tired herself, Shea went in search of Cynthia to say good-bye.

She finally spotted Kirsten's stepmother on the deck near the pool. She started through the sliding glass doors, then pulled back as she realized Cynthia and Kevin were in the midst of a heated private discussion, not a good time to interrupt. She was about to slip away when something Kevin said caught her ear.

"Disinherited? Over a stupid accident that wasn't even my fault?" His handsome face was flushed with anger, his voice a bellow of rage.

"Not disinherited, honey." Cynthia spoke calmly, but the nervous movements of her long, pink-tipped fingers betrayed her. "What your father is considering is a trust. You'd still have the income."

"But I couldn't touch the principal until I was thirty!" Kevin shouted. "That's unfair, Mother, and you know it."

"Yes, darling, I agree."

"Dad's just using the fender bender last night as an excuse to screw me out of my fair share of the inheritance."

"Don't blame your father. Blame Kirsten," Cynthia said.

Shea clutched the edge of the door so tightly, the tendons in her hands stood out like the ribs of a fan.

"Kirsten?"

"She always could wind her father around her little finger." Cynthia spoke bitterly. "But don't worry, Kevin. Nobody's going to cheat my children of what's rightfully theirs. Especially not the long-lost daughter." Cynthia's voice was scarcely more than a whisper, but it frightened Shea as no shout could have.

Shea slid the door shut quietly. Her fingers felt numb from having gripped it so tightly. She flexed them a time or two to restart the circulation, then turned back into the room, only to be brought up short by the sight of Ruth Griffin standing a few feet away.

A nasty, malicious, and distinctly un-Christian smirk twisted her plain features into a gargoylelike mask. "Eavesdroppers seldom hear any good of themselves," she said.

Shea brushed past her. "Tell my stepmother I had to leave."

The gloating sound of Ruth's laughter followed her from the room.

Teague took Shea to La Paloma, his favorite Mexican restaurant. She eyed the dingy cinder-block exterior with suspicion but seemed to relax once inside.

"Piñatas!" she said in delight, pointing to the colorful assortment hanging from the rafters.

As usual, the place was packed. "You *do* like Mexican, don't you?" he asked belatedly.

She blinked. "I guess so. Taco Bell counts, right?"

"Close enough." Teague caught the attention of the plump, middle-aged hostess.

She smiled and nodded in recognition, setting her long silver earrings jangling. "Senor Harris. Reservation for two, no?"

Teague nodded.

"Follow me, please." The woman moved quickly, dodging between the crowded tables, deftly avoiding collisions with the numerous white-shirted waiters. She seated them across from each other in a high-backed wooden booth at the very back of the restaurant, then brought them tall glasses of ice water and big handwritten menus.

"What would you like?" Teague asked.

Shea shrugged as she studied the menu in confusion. "I took only one year of Spanish. What are chongos?"

"A custardlike dessert with cinnamon sauce."

"Sounds great, but not for a main course. Why don't you order for me? Then if I don't like it, I'll have someone to blame besides myself."

"All right," he agreed, the corners of his mouth twitching.

"Watch it, Teague. You almost smiled there for a minute."

"What are you talking about? I smile."

"Oh, yeah? When?"

"I'm smiling now."

"That's not a smile; it's a smirk."

Their waiter introduced himself as Javier. He and Teague got into a heavy discussion of the relative merits of pescado a la Veracruzano and mole poblano de guajalote, both specialties of the house.

"Oh, go for the mole," Shea said. "At least I can pronounce it."

"Excellent choice," Javier said approvingly. He whisked away the menus and appeared moments later with a basket of tortilla chips, a bowl of salsa, and two bottles of beer.

Following Teague's lead, Shea dipped a chip into the chunky salsa, then took a tentative bite. "Tell me," she said. "What exactly is that mole whatever we ordered?"

"Turkey cooked with chocolate sauce," he told her, then choked on his beer at the expression on her face.

"Turkey with chocolate sauce? You did say *turkey* with chocolate sauce?"

"Don't worry. You'll like it. They use unsweetened chocolate. It's spicy, not sweet."

She ate another chip, then tried a cautious sip of the beer. When she made a face at the unfamiliar taste, Teague laughed out loud.

"I take it you're no beer drinker."

"You take it right. I'll stick to water, thanks." She leaned forward and he caught a tantalizing glimpse of white lace and soft, creamy skin. "Teague, I overheard a conversation this afternoon. Kevin and Cynthia were discussing the changes Jack plans to make in his will."

"And?" What was she getting at?

"Kevin was furious because his father intends to tie his inheritance up in a trust."

"He'll get over it." He took her hand. "And Jack'll probably change his mind once he calms down. They go through this same routine every time Kevin's in an accident."

"But he claims it wasn't his fault this time."

"It's never his fault," he said. "In this case, he shouldn't have parked so close to the other car."

"But his date said the space next to them was empty when they parked."

"Right. Only what Kevin didn't tell her was that he left the club to go buy condoms, and when he got back, he found that Walsh had pulled in on a diagonal, taking up a third of the adjacent parking space. Kevin managed to squeeze in. Unfortunately, Walsh wasn't as adept at squeezing out."

"So why didn't Kevin just park somewhere else?"

"I asked him the same thing. He said he didn't want Chelsea to realize he'd moved the car."

"He didn't want to explain where he'd been," she said.

"Right. Anyway, don't worry about Kevin. Believe me, Cynthia will make certain he's not slighted."

She shuddered. "You should have heard her. She can be a little scary, huh?"

"Ruthless when her children's interests are threatened," he agreed. "Kirsten never trusted her."

Shea frowned. "So what if she hires an investigator? It wouldn't take ten minutes to discover I'm not really Kirsten."

He drew ever-narrowing concentric circles in the palm of her hand. "Don't worry. I've already taken the proper CYA measures."

"Meaning?"

"I talked to Sheriff Carlton, told him the whole story, the true story."

"And he's going along with it?" Her voice rose.

"He wasn't happy about our little deception at first, but like me, the sheriff thinks the real Kirsten's dead, and he's as anxious as I am to flush out the killer."

"He's not worried that I'm a con artist who intends to cheat the Raineys?"

"He checked you out, Shea. No criminal record, not even a speeding ticket. You're just what you told me you were, a junior executive with a plastics firm in Ohio. At least you were until the company downsized a few months ago."

She didn't look at him, but he could feel the sudden tension in her hand.

"Want to tell me about that?"

"Not particularly, but since you already seem to know half the story . . ." She shrugged. "I went to work for Plas-Tech straight out of college. Jerry Maxwell, the owner, was a terrific boss. But when he retired eighteen months ago, his son Jason took over." She paused.

"Not such a terrific boss?"

"Oh, great boss. Lousy boyfriend. He's the colleague I mentioned dating. When we broke up, I was corporate history. Jason called it downsizing, but that was just an excuse."

Teague's eyebrows slammed together in a frown. "You didn't fight it?"

"My parents urged me to, but it seemed pointless. I didn't want to work with Jason any more than he wanted to work with me." She sighed. "Maybe I was wrong. I don't know. Water under the bridge now."

"And it's not like you have to work," he said.

She met his gaze. "Meaning?"

"The sheriff also learned that you inherited some money recently. Enough money to make it unlikely that you're a gold digger after a stake in the Rainey fortune."

She didn't look at him, but he could feel tension in her fingers again.

"What's wrong?" he asked.

"Nothing."

"You're upset because the sheriff ran a background check on you."

She looked up. "I know it's silly. He'd have been criminally negligent not to investigate my past."

"But?"

She dropped her gaze. "But I still feel violated. The way you must have felt last night when you discovered someone had been going through your things."

"I'm sorry, Shea, but we had to be sure you were telling the truth." He squeezed her hand. "Fact is, the sheriff's still following up on a couple of leads, trying to find a connection between you and the Raineys."

She frowned. "So he does suspect me of something?"

"Only of being related to Jack."

She smiled faintly, playing with the locket around her neck. "I've suspected that myself."

Javier brought their food then, and Teague watched in secret amusement as Shea took her first cautious bite.

"Oh, it's good!" she said, sounding surprised. "But spicy," she added, as the subtle fire of the mole sauce kicked in and she reached for her water glass. By the time she was finished, Teague knew where the evening was headed. Or at least where he hoped it was headed. He couldn't quit staring at her, and after a while he quit trying.

For dessert Javier brought fruit and a basket of tiny, nut-flavored Mexican wedding cookies.

"I really shouldn't," she said, but managed to nibble her way through a plate of fruit and two cookies. As she was reaching for a third, she glanced up and caught him looking at her. "Why do you do that?" she demanded.

"Do what?" he asked, trying to sound innocent.

"Stare."

"I like to watch you eat."

She grinned. "I've always had a healthy appetite. Fortunately, I'm blessed with a heavy-duty metabolism as well. Otherwise, I'd be big as a barn by now. Or at least a barnyard animal."

"You look perfect to me."

"You're not so bad yourself." Their gazes locked, and slowly her smile faded.

He reached across the table to rub a dusting of confectioner's sugar off her lower lip. Then he very deliberately sucked the sweet white powder off his fingertip.

She licked her trembling lower lip, her eyes luminous. "Teague?" she whispered.

In the background, recorded mariachi music competed with the clink of silverware and the chatter of the other customers. He wanted her, he thought, and unless he was crazy, she wanted him too. "Let's get out of here."

Shea breathed deeply, trying to calm her raging hormones. The cool night air helped to blunt the edge of the strange, dizzying euphoria possessing her, but when Teague took her arm to help her into the passenger seat of his pickup, another, even more powerful wave of emotion swept over her, weakening her knees and annihilating her inhibitions.

He got in on the driver's side. "Where to now? It's still early, but in Liberty our options are limited."

"Limited to what?" She leaned back against the headrest.

"A couple of bars on Main Street and a strip joint on the edge of town."

"No thanks."

"There's a movie theater, but the last show started at nine. You don't want to go in in the middle, do you?"

"No. What do you suggest?"

He turned to face her. She was very aware of his nearness in the confines of the front seat. "You could come to my apartment and look at my exquisite collection of—"

"Etchings?" The giddiness escaped in a giggle.

"Arrowheads, I was going to say, but I suppose it amounts to the same thing."

"The lodge is closer," she said, surprising herself. "Even though I don't have an arrowhead collection, exquisite or otherwise." She could, however, think of one or two other things to show him.

Teague's eyes gleamed as if he'd read her mind. "The lodge it is."

SEVEN

Inviting Teague back to her room was completely out of character. Normally Shea was wary of new relationships. But then normally a kiss didn't turn her brain to Silly Putty.

She leaned against the door of her room, digging in her purse for the key. "There's a hot tub on the deck," she heard herself say in a low, breathy voice. "Why don't we get comfortable out there, count stars or something. . . ." She trailed off. "I forgot. You don't have a swimsuit with you."

He studied her face in the light from the fixture above the door. The longer he stared without saying anything, the warmer her cheeks grew. She hoped she didn't look as nakedly needy as she felt.

He leaned closer, outlined her lips with a gentle forefinger, then kissed her once, softly. "Doesn't bother me," he said.

What didn't bother him? she wondered, having lost

the thread of the conversation in a maze of bewildering emotions.

Behind her, inside the cabin, the phone began to ring. She ignored it, willing Teague to kiss her again. She loved the touch of his lips, warm and tender, against her own.

He squeezed her hand. "You really ought to answer that."

She sighed in resignation and forced her heavy eyelids open. "It's probably a wrong number."

"You'll never know unless you open the door."

She fumbled the key, all thumbs under his watchful eyes.

"Here." He took the key from her, fitted it easily into the keyhole, and turned it smoothly in the lock.

The phone was on its fifth ring. She slipped past him to grab the receiver before the caller gave up. "Hello?"

"Who is it?" Teague asked as he pulled the door shut.

She waved him to silence. "Yes. What's wrong?" Shea froze as her caller's concern communicated itself across the phone lines.

"What's going on?" he asked again. She shook her head and held a finger to her lips.

"He's right here. We just got back from dinner."

"Who is it?" he mouthed silently.

"Cynthia." She held out the phone. "She wants to talk to you." Her face was bleak. Even though Kirsten's stepmother hadn't said much, Shea could tell the news was not good.

She stumbled over to the nearest chair and collapsed in a boneless heap. In a daze, she cradled her head in her hands, scarcely aware of the murmur of Teague's voice in the background. She didn't lift her gaze until the silence told her he had hung up.

"It's Jack, isn't it?"

He knelt in front of her chair and put his arms around her. There was no hint of the earlier sensuality in the gesture, just comfort. But the knowledge she saw mirrored in his gaze frightened her.

"About eight tonight," he said, "Jack complained of stomach pains. At first neither he nor Cynthia was particularly worried, but then he started to feel nauseous. When he began vomiting, Cynthia contacted the hospital. Somehow she and Mikey managed to get him out to the helicopter."

"Cynthia and Mikey? What about Kevin and the Griffins?"

"They'd left already."

"Left?"

"Yes. Kevin went out with friends. And the Griffins were at church."

"On a Wednesday night?"

"They're in a Bible study group." He paused. "Cynthia flew him straight to the emergency room."

"Oh, my God!" Her heart fluttered. She felt faint, but it wasn't until Teague shook her sharply that she realized she was still muttering "Oh, my God" over and over in a litany of fear. She choked to a halt. "Is he dead?" she asked, afraid to hear the answer.

Teague pulled her cold hands into his and held them tightly. "No, Cynthia said he's stable. Don't worry. Everything that can be done is being done."

She twisted her hands free. "Let's go to the hospital. I need to talk to Jack." She had to tell him the truth. Before it was too late.

Teague shook his head. "No. Jack's not in any shape to talk right now."

"But I can't sit around doing nothing," she protested, trying to get up.

He held her down. "Be still for a minute and listen. That's why Cynthia called. She needs your help. She hasn't been able to reach Kevin or the Griffins and she needs a baby-sitter. She wondered if you would take Mikey back to the island and stay with her, at least until someone else shows up to take charge."

"Sure. Of course I can do that. Is Mikey at the hospital with Cynthia and Jack?"

"Yeah." He nodded. "I said we'd be by to pick her up in a few minutes."

She frowned earnestly at the travel alarm clock on the bedside table. "I'd better pack a bag."

He let her up, and she went through the motions of packing like an automaton. "Do you think I'll need my jacket? No, not just for overnight," she answered herself. "How about my sunglasses? Should I take them?"

"The sun's been down for hours," he said.

She nodded. "You're right. I guess I'm not thinking very clearly."

"Are you ready?"

"I suppose." She surveyed the room doubtfully, wondering what essential item she was forgetting.

He gently bumped her chin with his fist. "Buck up, baby."

Shea felt a warning prickle behind her eyelids. "Oh, no. Don't be nice to me, Teague. I'll start crying, and I hate women who bawl all the time."

He shouldered her bag. "In that case, move it, Mc-

Kenzie. We don't have all night. How's that? Rude enough to suit you?"

Tossing him a grateful smile, she grabbed her purse. "Better."

They found Cynthia and Mikey playing tick-tack-toe in the waiting room nearest the emergency entrance. Mikey placed an "O" in the upper left corner of the grid. "Gotcha!" she said.

"Yes, you did, you little rascal. I'm stuck. Looks like the cat wins this game." Cynthia glanced up and noticed them. Her fine-boned face showed signs of strain. "Thank goodness you're here," she said. "I'm running out of activities to keep Mikey occupied. This place isn't set up to entertain children."

"Hi, Teague. Hi, Kirsten." Evidently the evening's drama had had little effect on the youngest Rainey. She appeared more excited than frightened.

"Hi, yourself," Shea said.

Teague tugged the little girl's ponytail. "We're gonna take you back to the island, shortcake."

"Yes!" she said, glomming on to Teague's legs in an enthusiastic hug.

"How's Daddy?" Shea was almost afraid to ask.

"He's sleeping now," Cynthia answered with a faint smile. "They think they treated him in time."

"What was it?" Teague asked. "Flu? Or his cancer taking a turn for the worse?"

"Didn't I tell you?" Cynthia stared from Shea to Teague in surprise. "The doctor says he was poisoned."

"Poisoned?" Teague's eyebrows collided. "Are they certain?"

"They won't know until they get the lab report back

on his stomach contents, but they're pretty sure it was a reaction to something he ate."

"Food poisoning?" Shea asked.

"Or poison in the food. The doctor I spoke to wouldn't hazard a guess which." She lifted her shoulders in a graceful gesture of denial. "Who would want to poison Jack?"

"Right offhand I can think of a dozen suspects," Teague said. "Jack's rich, and greed's a powerful motive."

Shea frowned at him. "Granted the money provides a motive, but why poison a man who's already mortally ill?"

"Kirsten's right, Teague. You're jumping to conclusions. It must have been an accident."

But Teague wasn't ready to give up. "What did Jack eat today? What medicines did he take?"

Cynthia looked bewildered. "His IV. No medicine other than that. And very little food. All I was able to coax down him was some eggnog this morning and a little soup for dinner. Neither should have upset his stomach."

Teague frowned. "No point worrying about it, I guess. We'll just have to wait for the lab report."

"Is there anything we can do to help?" Shea felt useless.

"Just keep an eye on Mikey for me. This isn't a good place for her right now. She's better off on the island."

Teague patted Cynthia's shoulder reassuringly. "Don't worry. Kirsten and I will take good care of her."

"And if there's any change or if you need something, just give us a call," Shea added.

Cynthia hugged the three of them good-bye, then waved them out of sight. Shea felt guilty about leaving her there alone even though it was apparently what she wanted.

"I'm hungry," Mikey announced as she buckled herself into the middle seat of Teague's pickup.

"Me too," Teague agreed. "How does a hot fudge sundae sound? I know a place that serves great sundaes. Huge mounds of ice cream drowning in oceans of hot fudge and topped with real whipped cream."

"At this time of night?" Shea asked. It sounded like a recipe for indigestion.

"All right!" Mikey's enthusiasm overruled her.

"Don't you think she ought to be in bed?" Shea protested.

"Actually," Teague said with a wink, "that's where *I* was planning to be right about now." He moved his eyebrows up and down like the lecherous villain of a melodrama.

Shea laughed. "Okay. Hot fudge sundaes it is." Chocolate was the next best thing. Or so she'd heard.

Mikey's eyes began to droop about halfway through her sundae. By the time they made the crossing to the island, she was sound asleep.

Shea clambered onto the dock first. Then Teague carefully handed the gently snoring child across to her. Shouldering Shea's duffel bag, Teague leaped onto the weathered boards of the dock. He checked the luminous face of his watch. "It's only eleven. Seems later, doesn't it?"

It did. Shea breathed deeply of the night air. Moonlight painted silver squiggles on the surface of the lake.

Teague took Mikey from her. "Shortcake's heavier than she looks, huh?"

Shea nodded in heartfelt agreement. Forty-odd

pounds of sleeping child would have been quite a load for her to haul across the island. She was thankful Teague had elected to help. Even he looked relieved as the house came into view.

Not surprisingly, considering the circumstances under which Cynthia had left the island, lights blazed from every window and the doors were unlocked.

"Where's Mikey's bedroom, I wonder?"

"Upstairs," Shea said. "Next to Kirsten's."

Slowly she trailed Teague up the broad staircase to the second floor, uneasily aware of a prickling sensation on the back of her neck. If she hadn't known better, she'd have sworn she was under surveillance.

"Kirsten?" she whispered softly. "Are you here?"

"Did you say something?" Teague glanced back at her over his shoulder.

"No, nothing important."

She followed him into Mikey's room. Cynthia's flair for decorating was evident in the bright palette of primary colors. A huge rocking horse stood in one corner. The low shelves that ran along the window wall were packed with toys, notably a huge collection of Legos and enough teddy bears to stock a big city Toys "Я" Us.

Shea pulled down the covers on the four-poster, and Teague settled Mikey on the mattress. The little girl slept so soundly that she didn't stir, even when Shea removed her shoes and tucked her in.

They tiptoed out, closing the door quietly behind them.

Teague stopped outside Kirsten's door. "You've had a shock. Maybe you should get some sleep too," he suggested.

"In Kirsten's room?" She cast a doubtful look at the

closed door. Her reluctance bordered on fear. "It's locked, isn't it? Per Jack's orders?"

"With Kirsten back he changed the order."

"Are you sure? No one said anything to me."

"I heard him tell Ruth myself." He studied her face carefully. "You're not afraid to sleep in Kirsten's room, are you?"

"Not afraid exactly." She couldn't meet his gaze. "But I can't help feeling like an intruder."

He took her by the arm, tilting her face up to his. "It's more than that. What are you so scared of, Shea? Ghosts?" He must have felt the reaction that went shivering through her because his expression changed, sharpened. "Ghosts?" he repeated.

"No, of course not. Don't be ridiculous." She twisted away.

"Ghosts aren't real, Shea."

"Kirsten's memories—"

He dismissed her argument with a wave of his hand. "I don't know where these so-called memories are coming from, but I'm sure there's a rational explanation for it."

"Like what?"

"Like maybe you have extragood intuition. Or maybe it's coincidence. But the supernatural? I don't think so."

Her face must have revealed her doubts.

"Okay, look. I'll prove to you there's nothing spooky about Kirsten's room." He turned the doorknob. Or tried to. It was locked.

A wave of relief swept over her at the sudden reprieve. "I guess Ruth isn't too good at following orders."

"There must be a key around here somewhere," he said.

He headed downstairs, and she followed him slowly, trailing her fingers along the smooth wood of the bannister. A sudden sound startled her. She paused, cocking her head to listen. "Did you hear that, Teague?"

"Hear what?" He glanced back up at her from the bottom of the stairs, a questioning expression on his face.

She shook her head. "Nothing, I guess. For a minute I thought I heard a humming sound, but it's gone now." She shook her head again. But as Teague turned away, she heard it again, not a sound so much as a vibration, which seemed to tingle through the soles of her feet, through the fingers resting lightly on the bannister.

Shea stared at the polished wood, suddenly aware that she knew exactly how it felt to sling a leg over it and slide down backward, the thrill of the forbidden ride followed by an abrupt jolt as she butted up against the heavy newel post at the bottom. "Kirsten?" she whispered.

The humming grew to a veritable roar, yet Teague appeared to hear nothing out of the ordinary. He stood with his back toward her, searching through a brass bowl of odds and ends on the living-room mantel. The roaring in her ears built to a crescendo, drowning her in a powerful and disturbing wave of déjà vu.

The last time she'd seen Teague standing by the mantel, he'd been waiting for her, waiting to take her to a party at the club. She'd been wearing a little black dress, the one Daddy had threatened to burn.

She'd paused halfway down the stairs, willing Teague to turn, knowing that he would, and that when he did, the look on his face would be worth every penny she'd spent on the dress.

He turned, then seemed to freeze for one endless moment. The look on his face wasn't quite what she'd expected. Instead of appreciation and desire, there was incredulity and shock.

"Kirsten?" he said in a ragged voice. He blinked, then blinked again, as if he couldn't believe his eyes. "Shea? What is this? A joke?"

She didn't answer, though her gaze never left his for an instant. All her attention was focused on his beloved face. She couldn't get enough of looking at him.

She seemed to float down the stairs and into his arms, her body as insubstantial as a dream. Still in that strange somnambulist state, she dragged his face down to hers and kissed him with all the force of her long-pent-up passion. Seven long years she'd hungered for this. Seven endless years lost in a limbo of yearning.

Teague drew back with a startled look. "Shea?" he whispered.

Kirsten smiled at him with Shea's mouth and Shea's dimple. "No, silly." She pouted prettily. "Don't you recognize me, Wolfman?"

His blood ran cold. He stared at her, still not believing.

She stiffened and frowned slightly. "You're not happy to see me?"

"I—" *Happy* wasn't the right word.

"I know I'm trespassing, but I had to say good-bye. Things ended so abruptly for me. For us." Her mouth tightened. "I was murdered, Teague. The murderer has to pay." She closed her eyes for a second. Then her eyelids fluttered open again and she sighed softly. "I've missed you."

It's not really Kirsten, he told himself. For some bizarre reason, Shea must be trying to trick him. He gripped her shoulders. "This isn't funny."

"It's not meant to be." Although her lips were curved in a gentle smile, her eyes were tragic. She ran the back of her hand along his cheek. "Must be a full moon," she whispered.

His guts tied themselves in knots. "This can't be. *You* can't be," he protested.

The look on her face was inexpressibly sad. "Can't it? 'There are more things in heaven and earth,'" she quoted, then smiled ruefully. "Despite all the lies and the trickery, I truly did love you, Teague." She kissed the tip of one finger, then pressed it to his lips. "Good-bye, Wolfman."

Teague started to say something, but before he had a chance to utter a word, her face went blank and she crumpled, going limp in his arms like a marionette with broken strings.

When Shea regained consciousness, she was alone, stretched out on the sofa in front of the fireplace and wrapped in the soft folds of a mohair afghan. The hands of the grandfather clock stood at five after four. She'd been asleep for several hours.

"Teague?" she called. Her voice seemed to echo in the silence.

She sat up in a rush as she remembered the events immediately preceding her collapse. Had it been a dream? Surely it had. She couldn't have done what she'd done, said what she'd said. It wasn't possible, was it?

"Teague?" She could hear the rising panic in her voice. Surely, *surely*, it had been a dream. She'd been thinking about Kirsten earlier, had been uneasy about trespassing in Kirsten's room. Perhaps those brooding thoughts had triggered her strange dream.

She heard him coming before she saw him. "Shea, it's all right. I'm here." He ran down the stairs.

She struggled to put her fears into words. "I-I didn't know where you were." That sounded pretty lame. She sat up straighter, gripping her hands together tightly. "I had a bad dream. When I woke up, you were gone."

"Not gone. I've been here all along. I just slipped upstairs for a minute to check on Mikey. She's fine, by the way, snoring away like a buzz saw. I didn't know kids could rip zees like that." He edged closer, and she saw the wary expression in his eyes, so at odds with his casual tone.

Her throat tightened. "It wasn't a dream, was it?"

He didn't say anything, but that was a kind of answer in itself.

Sinking down next to her, he wrapped his arms around her. She had an almost overpowering urge to dissolve against him in a soggy puddle of emotion, but she didn't. She searched his face for the truth. "Teague, am I going crazy?"

"If you are, then apparently it's a contagious form of madness."

She grabbed him by the shirtfront as if she were a cop and he were an uncooperative witness. "Tell me what you saw!"

He gathered her hands in his, holding them against

his heart, which was pounding away beneath his shirt like a jackhammer. "I saw Kirsten. I looked up and there she was, staring at me through your eyes."

"My God, Teague, what's going on?" Her voice was a hoarse whisper.

"I'm not sure. Group hallucination?"

"Do you think so?" she asked hopefully. "I was afraid I'd been possessed, that it was only a matter of time before I saw my face plastered all over the covers of supermarket tabloids." She felt edgy, restive, as if an electric charge were building in the room. She rubbed distractedly at her arms and was surprised to see the fine hairs standing on end.

"Do you remember what happened?" he asked.

Shea nodded. "She was in charge, but I was there— seeing, hearing, *feeling* everything."

He gripped her shoulders. "Feeling what?"

"Joy at seeing you again after so long. Remorse for things she'd never be able to change. And underneath . . ."

"What?" He tightened his grip. His expression was strained, his eyes like chips of flint.

"Anger," she said quietly. "A cold, implacable anger."

"Anger?" His voice rose. "Kirsten's angry with me?"

She shrugged his hands away, drew her knees up, and hugged them to her chest. "I don't know. I don't think so. What I sensed was more like a background emotion without any specific focus." She shrugged again. "She was angry, but I don't know with whom. I'm not sure she knows."

He stood and began pacing the room. "Before Kirsten took over, did you have any warning? Or was it like the 'memories,' just there without your realizing anything extraordinary had happened?"

Shea cocked her head to one side, remembering. "I heard a low hum."

"A hum?"

"A vibration really, hard to describe."

"I didn't hear anything."

"Glory said she didn't, either."

"You heard this noise before when Glory was with you?"

"Yes, when we were hauling the photo albums down from the attic. I heard a similar noise then that seemed to be coming from Kirsten's room. Only Glory claimed she didn't hear it. I thought she was lying."

"Why would she do that?"

"Because she'd accidentally locked Beelzebub inside Kirsten's room. I thought she was afraid she'd get in trouble. You know what her mother's like."

"Yes."

Shea frowned. "What's going on, Teague?"

He leaned against the mantel, rubbing his forehead as if it hurt. "I wish I knew. Ghostly visitations. Possession." He gave a bark of unamused laughter. "Not topics I've given much thought to. I keep thinking there must be a logical explanation."

"What happened tonight scared me. I was out of control. No." She gazed at him helplessly, then shook her head and tried again, struggling to define the difference more exactly. "I was there, conscious of everything that was happening, but Shea wasn't in control of the situation. *I* was in control, but *I* wasn't Shea. For a little while I was Kirsten. I was Kirsten!" She stared at him, round-eyed.

Teague resumed his pacing. "There must be a logical explanation."

"What? We're both nuts?"

"Nah, unlikely." One of his rare smiles softened the harsh contours of his face. "But I'm not convinced you're possessed, either, whatever the hell that means."

A muscle in her face twitched uncontrollably. "Then how do you explain—"

"What I said before—hallucination. It was late. Tired, stressed out, we were both in a highly suggestible state. After all the time you spent preparing for the masquerade, it's hardly surprising that in a state of lowered resistance, you got a little mixed-up, identified too closely."

She wasn't convinced his theory was the correct one, but she didn't feel like arguing anymore. "Maybe," she said. Though it didn't explain his experience.

"Right now what we both need most is sleep."

Good idea. With a little luck, she might wake up to find this whole mess had been a nightmare.

EIGHT

Shea slept fitfully, plagued by nightmares, though the only one she remembered clearly was the one that woke her. She flew off the sofa like a rock from a slingshot, positive she was being chased by a freak with a chain saw. The scary part was that even after she was awake, she could still hear the chain saw roaring away. It took almost a full minute for her brain to accept the fact that it was just someone vacuuming a nearby room.

Teague had left a note propped against the brass bowl on the mantel. According to this brief missive Cynthia—and presumably Kevin—were still at the hospital, and Teague was at the job site.

Shea checked on Mikey. The little girl was still sound asleep, not surprising since it was only six-forty. Evidently the mad vacuumer hadn't been at work up there yet.

Armed with scouring powder and toilet bowl cleaner, Glory Griffin burst in on Shea just as she was stepping out of the shower. "I'm sorry," mumbled the embarrassed girl, looking away.

Shea wrapped herself in an oversize bath towel. "My fault. I thought the door was locked."

"I'll come back later," Glory said. "I didn't mean to barge in on you. Mama told me to start with this bathroom. Usually I do the upstairs first."

"I see." And she did; Ruth was playing games.

"The schedule's off today because Mr. Jack's gone. Normally I can't even run the vacuum until after ten."

If the Griffins knew that Jack had been rushed to the hospital, then Ruth had darn well known that Shea was trying to sleep downstairs when she'd ordered Glory to rev up the vacuum cleaner. The woman was a menace.

Shea dressed, then headed for the kitchen, wondering what surprises Ruth had planned to enliven her breakfast. Orange juice in a dribble cup? An exploding toaster?

Mikey was perched on a stool at the counter downing her cereal with the same enthusiasm she had shown for her sundae the night before.

"That looks pretty good," Shea said. "I'll have the same, Ruth."

The housekeeper glanced up from the sink, where she was sorting raspberries, and smirked. "Sorry. No more milk."

"Great." Shea studied the other woman. Ruth's fat face looked smug. Had she deliberately used the last of the milk so there wouldn't be enough for Shea's breakfast? It seemed the sort of petty behavior she specialized in.

She peered through the contents of the big refrigerator. "No problem. I'll just scramble myself an egg."

"No eggs, either."

"Toast?"

"No bread."

"Okay," Shea said, tiring of the game. "What *can* I have for breakfast?"

"There's some prune juice in the refrigerator. And there's plenty of cereal. Of course, like I said, the milk's all gone."

First the vacuum cleaner, now this. Shea ground her teeth. "At least if I don't eat anything," she said under her breath, "I don't have to worry about being poisoned."

"Poisoned?" The housekeeper froze. "What's that supposed to mean?"

"Didn't Cynthia tell you what the doctor said?" If Cynthia hadn't said anything to Ruth, maybe she'd had a reason. Shea wished she'd kept her mouth shut.

The older woman scowled, but her anger couldn't entirely mask the shadow of fear in her eyes. "Why don't you fill me in?"

If Ruth was the one who'd poisoned Jack, she already knew more than Shea did, and if she was innocent, then what would it hurt to tell her? "Daddy was poisoned by something he ingested."

"Ingested?"

"Ate."

"I didn't poison him!" Ruth protested quickly. Too quickly?

"I never suggested you did."

"You said Mr. Jack was poisoned by something he ate, and I'm the cook." Her voice rose shrilly.

Shea eyed the housekeeper warily. Why was she so worked up? Unless . . .

A muscle twitched beneath Ruth's left eye. "I had no

reason to poison Mr. Jack. How could anybody believe I'd do such a wicked thing?"

She edged around the housekeeper. "Ruth, no one's accused you of anything."

The housekeeper crushed a handful of berries in one fat fist. The juice dripped through her fingers like blood. Slowly she turned on Shea. "You're the one," she said, her face twisted, her eyes wild. "You did it! You're here to murder us all!" Her voice spiraled into a scream.

Mikey's face paled.

The woman fell heavily to her knees, locking her pudgy hands together like a set of vise grips. Berry juice dripped down her arms. "Lord of lords, king of kings, this humble servant implores thee. Preserve us from the murdering impostor."

"She's not a nimposter," Mikey said. "She's Kirsten."

Ruth's eyes were bloodshot and distended. Prominent veins writhed like snakes beneath the skin of her sweaty, flushed forehead. "Miss Kirsten's dead. I saw her." She threw both arms in the air. "As God is my witness, I saw her poor white face staring up from the pit." Spittle glistened at the corners of her mouth. She turned an accusing glare on Shea. "God will punish the wicked. You'll burn in hell for what you've done!"

Mikey ran out, but Shea stood, transfixed, both fascinated and repulsed.

Alerted by the sound of her mother's shrill invective, Glory burst into the room. She teetered in the doorway, halting at the sight of Ruth kneeling on the kitchen floor, her arms raised to heaven in supplication.

"Mama? Are you all right?"

Ruth ran through another impassioned prayer or two,

then groaned and collapsed, still raving, but with the volume tuned down to an unintelligible mumble.

Glory turned a worried face to Shea. "What happened? What did she say?"

Shea shrugged. "She swears I can't be Kirsten because she saw Kirsten at the bottom of a pit."

Glory shook her head in despair. "It's that dream she had when you were first kidnapped. She can't accept the fact her vision was only a nightmare. That's why she's been so nasty to you. I apologize, Miss Kirsten." She turned to her mother. "Mama, you're gonna make yourself sick if you keep this up. Come home and lie down for a while."

Feeling sick and shaken, Shea slipped out the back door to the deck. Ruth Griffin wasn't just a menace; she was an unbalanced menace. No, worse than that. She was stark raving mad. Shea hoped she hadn't screwed up. If the housekeeper had, indeed, poisoned Jack for whatever insane reason, then she hadn't done the authorities any favor by tipping the woman off.

Mikey edged through the sliding glass doors onto the deck, casting a cautious glance back over her shoulder as if she was afraid of being followed. "Where's Ruth?" she whispered. She was still wearing the clothes she had slept in, her hair was full of knots, and she had a milk mustache.

"I'm not doing a very good job of looking after you, am I, Mikey?" Shea brushed the tangled curls back out of the little girl's face. "Don't worry. Glory took her mom home to rest for a while. Does Ruth flip out like that very often?"

"Sometimes," Mikey said. "It scares me."

Shea nodded. "Me too."

"Do you think maybe she was the one who poisoned Daddy?"

"We don't know for sure that anyone poisoned Daddy. Maybe he just got ahold of some bad food. You don't believe Ruth would hurt Daddy on purpose, do you?"

Mikey studied her bare feet as if the key to Ruth Griffin's twisted personality might be hiding between her toes. "No, I guess not. She likes Daddy pretty much. I'm not so sure about Beelzebub, though. Ruth called him a limb of Satan just 'cause he tracked mud on the floor. She might have poisoned *him*." Her grave observation was laced with sadness. She seemed to have abandoned the dognapping theory.

Wishing she'd never mentioned the word *poison* in the first place, Shea pulled Mikey into a tight hug. The little girl clung to her as if she were the only link to safety in a strange and dangerous world. "Don't worry. I'll protect you, little sister," Kirsten said. Shea didn't argue the point.

"What do you want to do today?" Shea asked as she combed the tangles from Mikey's freshly washed hair.

"Can you braid my hair like yours?"

"Sure. No problem. Are we going for the twin effect?"

"Yes," Mikey said. "I want to look just like you."

"You want to look like the nimposter?" Shea teased.

The child looked at her with a seriousness beyond her years. "I don't care if you're a nimposter or not. At least you don't act crazy."

Shea smiled at the vote of confidence. "You still haven't told me what you want to do, though."

"I want to go see Daddy."

Shea began plaiting the girl's soft dark hair into a French braid. "Me too. We can do that later, but I meant this morning. Are there any special places on the island I haven't seen yet?"

Mikey considered the question. "The old cabin," she said at last, "where the massacre took place."

"Sounds like fun." Shea grimaced. At least more fun than she'd had so far today.

Teague spotted Shea and Mikey toiling up through the meadow toward him. A swallowtail flittered past Shea's nose, then landed on a lacy frond of wild parsley. The trill of a meadowlark floated on the morning air above the low murmur of the creek.

"What are you two up to this morning?" he asked.

Shea's smile put a hitch in his breathing. "Exploring," she told him.

"I'm taking Kirsten to see the old cabin," Mikey said.

"Don't go inside. The floorboards are probably rotted out. You'd break your neck if you fell through into the cellar."

Shea gave a thumbs-up. "Fine with me. I personally steer clear of small, dark buildings. They tend to aggravate my raging claustrophobia."

"Nothing to see, anyway," Mikey told her. "Kevin moved all the good stuff a long time ago."

"What good stuff?" Teague asked.

"My rock collection," Shea said. "Ruth wouldn't let me keep it in the house. Too messy."

Was that Kirsten speaking? Or Shea? Teague raised an eyebrow. "I'm taking a break, anyway. Mind if I tag along?"

Mikey let out a whoop of approval, then took off full speed toward the trees.

"Second that motion." At close range, Shea's smile was a lethal weapon.

Teague's heart stopped, then restarted in higher gear. He tugged her into his arms almost roughly, doing his best to kiss her as senseless as he was.

"C'mon, you guys!" Mikey urged, obviously impatient with their lollygagging.

Teague was surprised when he broke the kiss and discovered he could lift his lips from Shea's. He'd have sworn the heat had fused their mouths together.

Shea's eyelids flickered open and she gazed up at him with a lazy smile. "Now that," she said, "makes up for my lousy morning."

"C'mon!" Mikey yelled.

"We're coming!" he said.

They followed Mikey, picking their way carefully among the wild strawberries that thrived as ground cover under the big ponderosas. The air was heavy with the sweet scent of ripening berries and the fragrance of pine. The setting was idyllic, so when a chipmunk ran across their path, scolding them for the intrusion, and Shea flinched, he was surprised. He put a hand on her arm. "What is it? What's wrong?" Her muscles felt taut.

"I don't know. Nothing, I guess. Nothing reasonable, anyway. I'm fighting a strong compulsion to turn tail and run."

They were heading downhill now as the path paralleled the little spring. The water rippled over the rocks, though it was hidden from sight by the thick under-growth that hemmed the banks of the creek. The trees thinned as the path led closer to the shore, but even though the going was easier, Shea's steps slowed, then stopped altogether.

"What is it?" Teague asked again.

"Just admiring the view." She waved a hand like a tour guide pointing out the high points, the sparkling cobalt waters of Crescent Lake, the majestic mountains of the Bitterroot range. But her hand shook, and her eyes were wary.

A thicket of alders lay directly ahead. Mikey paused at the edge of the tangle, urging them on, but Shea seemed to be rooted to the spot. Eyes wide and frightened, she stared at the thicket. Her hands trembled; her breathing was harsh and unsteady.

"Shea, what's wrong?" This reaction was even more violent than the one that had immobilized her during their stroll along the shore. She shot him an anguished look.

He felt his own skin prickle as he realized this was the same spot that had put her hackles up before. They were approaching from a different angle this time, but it was the same dense copse of trees. What was going on?

The sound began as a low vibration that barely regis-tered on his consciousness. It soon grew into a rhythmic drone, then a persistent clatter so loud, it drowned out the thrum of blood in his veins. The helicopter flashed overhead like a giant insect, heading for the landing pad behind the house.

Mikey stopped to track its progress. "They're home," she yelled. "Let's go back."

Shea sagged with a relief so intense, she would have landed on her knees if he hadn't grabbed her arm.

Switching directions, they headed back. Fifteen minutes later, hot and out of breath, they reached the house.

"Daddy?" Mikey flew through the sliding glass doors. "Daddy?" Shea and Teague were right behind her.

Cynthia appeared at the head of the stairs.

"Mom!" Mikey launched herself up the steps. Cynthia rocked back under the onslaught but managed to keep her feet.

"Hold on, honey. What's your hurry?"

"Is Daddy back?"

Cynthia detached Mikey and knelt down so that their faces were on the same level. "No, he's still too weak to leave the hospital, but he's better. The doctor says the danger is over."

"When can I see him?" Mikey asked. Her voice quavered.

Cynthia shot a look of entreaty at Teague and Shea, the strain evident on her face. "Could you take her to the hospital this afternoon, Kirsten? I'm sure you're anxious to see your father too. He's been asking about both of you."

"He's conscious then?"

"In and out. Sleeping a lot. This attack used up most of his reserves. You won't be able to stay long, but I know he'd like to see you."

"We'll head over then—about four if that's all right," Shea said.

"Perfect." Cynthia frowned. "Where's Ruth? When I got back, the house was empty."

"She had one of her fits," Mikey told her mother solemnly.

"Oh, terrific. That's all I need right now. I should have insisted that Jack fire her years ago." She sighed. "What incredibly inconvenient timing. I hate to ask, Kirsten, but could you stay with Mikey awhile longer? I don't feel safe leaving her in Ruth's care. Not under the circumstances. It would just be until Kevin's free to take over."

"Of course," Shea said. "Anything I can do to help."

"Have you talked to the police yet?" Teague asked.

"What?" Cynthia looked at him as if he were as loony as the housekeeper.

Shea caught on right away. "About Daddy. Last night you said the doctor suspected poisoning, but that he was waiting for the lab results."

Cynthia smiled faintly. "Can you believe it? I'd forgotten. Evidently the doctor's still waiting, because he hasn't said another word to me."

"No news is good news," Shea said. "I think. Have you seen Kevin? He didn't come home last night."

"I tracked him down at the club, and he spelled me at Jack's bedside last night. He's with Jack now."

Shea nodded. "Is there anything else we can do for you?"

"Pray."

"They moved Jack out of the ICU an hour ago." Cynthia looked ten years younger than she had earlier in the day.

"That's great news," Shea said. She and Mikey had come into town with Teague. Kevin was baby-sitting while Shea and Teague went out to dinner.

"When is Daddy coming home?" Mikey asked.

Cynthia ruffled her bangs. "Soon, honey." She took Mikey up to the maternity ward to see the babies, leaving Shea behind to visit with Jack.

He sat propped against the pillows, his pale eyes alert. "Have a seat," he croaked.

She pulled a chair close to his bed and sat down. "You sound terrible." Nearly as bad as he looked.

His smile was a ghastly rictus in his ravaged face. "They pumped my stomach. The equipment's rough on the throat."

Shea tried to smile but couldn't. "Oh, Daddy. I'm so sorry."

He nodded. "Me too. I guess I won't be eating any parsnip soup for a while."

"Is that what made you sick?"

"So the doctor said. Somehow a water hemlock root got mixed in with the parsnips."

"How could Ruth have made such a mistake?"

"Evidently hemlock looks—and tastes—like parsnips."

"Except hemlock's deadly." Perhaps Ruth had poisoned her employer on purpose. "Daddy?"

"What, baby?"

Shea wanted to ask him about the photo of her mother, but one glance at his haggard face and wasted body told her that now was not the time. She patted his hand. "Get better. The island's not the same without you."

As they worked their way through grilled sirloin and baked potatoes, Teague told Shea what he'd learned about Jack's poisoning.

"Could the hemlock in the soup have been an accident?" Shea asked.

"Maybe." He poked his steak. "There's a clump of the stuff growing right next to the Raineys' garden. Thing is, Hal knows the difference and swears he didn't pick any hemlock by mistake."

Shea frowned. "Maybe not. Or maybe he got careless and now he's in denial. Or—"

"Maybe he did it on purpose," he finished.

"Motive?"

"Gain. The promise of an inheritance."

"Pretty thin," she said. "Why take a chance murdering someone who's so close to death?"

"I didn't say I thought he was guilty, just that he was a suspect."

"Who else is a suspect?"

"Ruth. She made the soup."

She sighed heavily. "I'd like to believe it was her. She's not my favorite person." She stabbed viciously at a chunk of potato. "But . . ."

He nodded. "Just because she's a couple of bubbles off plumb, that doesn't mean she's a murderer."

"So who else could have done it?"

"There's always Cynthia."

"Cynthia?" Shea froze, the forkful of potato halfway to her mouth.

"The wife's always the number one suspect. She had motive and opportunity. Not only was she the one who ordered the parsnip soup, she was also the one who cleaned and chopped the parsnips."

"I thought Ruth did all the cooking."

"Normally she does, but yesterday Cynthia volunteered to get a jump on dinner preparations while Ruth changed Jack's sheets."

"But if Cynthia was guilty, she wouldn't have left such an obvious trail. She's too smart to incriminate herself," Shea said.

"I agree. And the fact is, anyone could have added a couple of hemlock roots to the pile of parsnips Hal left on the chopping block."

"Anyone?" she challenged.

"Anyone with access to the island. And that includes my crew, me, and you."

Shea choked on a bite of sirloin. "So now I'm a suspect too?"

"Hypothetically, everyone in Liberty is a suspect."

Shea wasn't sure why she'd asked Teague in when he brought her back to the lodge. No, that was a lie. She knew. She just didn't want to admit it, even to herself. "So," she said. Monosyllables hardly qualified as sparkling repartee, but the sight of him sprawled across one end of the loveseat on the far side of the room brought all nonessential brain activity to a screeching halt. She felt lucky to have managed anything more than a grunt.

Teague bunched a loose pillow behind his head. "Want to watch some TV?"

"Sure. I guess. What's on?" She kicked off her shoes and curled up in one of the armchairs on the opposite side of the room. She didn't trust her own control with her pesky hormones running amok. Not that she was averse to a few kisses and a lingering embrace or two, but she wasn't ready to commit to more than that, not until she knew for certain that Teague wasn't confusing her with Kirsten. The problem was, her body didn't have the same reservations that her mind had.

"Letterman okay?"

"Fine. Would you care for some coffee? I can call room service."

"Not right now. Why don't you move over here next to me?" He patted the loveseat in invitation. "You're going to get a stiff neck if you try to watch TV from that angle."

Better her with a stiff neck than him with a stiff . . . "I'm okay. Really."

"Yeah, but I'm giving myself a sore throat yelling across the room."

She made a face. "It's not *that* far. I'm not straining my voice at all."

"What?"

She tried to frown but couldn't control the twitch of her lips. "Very funny."

Teague yawned, stretched, and settled back against the throw pillow with a sigh of contentment.

"Don't you dare fall asleep, Teague Harris."

"Come keep me awake," he suggested, opening one eye.

"Forget it. If I went over there, the first thing you know we'd be kissing."

"That *would* be a tragedy." He laughed. "So if kissing's out, I guess cuddling's off limits too, huh?"

"Teague, I . . . What about Kirsten?"

"Kirsten has nothing to do with us."

"Us?" There was an *us*? Shea's heart raced.

Teague crossed the room in three strides. He tugged her out of the chair and into his arms. "Us," he said softly. "You and me."

"You and me?" Three whole syllables. Pretty good, considering that her brain had shorted out again.

He pulled her into a tighter embrace, one hand cupping the back of her head while the other rested in the small of her back. She looked into his eyes and felt as if she were drowning in their smoky depths. Her heart drummed madly. She slid her hands up the hard muscles of his back and felt the shudder of his response.

"I think I'm falling in love with you, Shea McKenzie." His voice was a ragged whisper in her ear.

Good thing, because I'm definitely falling in love with you, Teague Harris.

This time when he kissed her, it was different, as if they'd progressed to another level of intimacy. This kiss offered a promise, a challenge, and a passionate intensity that was almost frightening.

She gasped for breath when he released her. Her bloodstream was nine-tenths hormones. She couldn't have framed a coherent sentence if her life had depended on it.

"I want you, Shea, but you're not sure yet, are you?" His eyes had darkened to charcoal. They burned into hers.

"I . . ." she started, but the words refused to come. She clung to him desperately. "I—"

"Shh." Teague pressed a finger to her lips. "Don't say anything. It's all right. I'm a patient man." He pressed a final soft kiss to her forehead and was gone before she realized quite what had happened.

A cold shower helped, but not much. Shea kept picturing Teague naked in the shower with her, naked in the hot tub, naked in her bed. She paced back and forth in front of the French doors, trying to calm her fevered emotions.

Why had he left? That was the question that plagued her. She'd been ready to drop into his hands like a ripe peach. All right, so maybe there would have been some regrets in the morning, but it was a long time until morning.

She paced some more, hoping the management wouldn't bill her for the hole she was wearing in the carpet.

A cold shower helped, but not much. Teague kept picturing Shea naked in the shower with him, naked in the hot tub, naked in her bed. Dammit, why had he left? She'd been as aroused as he was. She wouldn't have refused him.

He sighed heavily. But she probably would have regretted her impulsive actions in the morning, and he didn't want that.

Too keyed up to sleep, he went for a swim. The icy water off the point soon chilled his fevered blood. He swam halfway to the island and back, until he was almost too tired to drag himself back up onto the dock and into bed.

Shea slept restlessly and woke early. After grabbing a quick bite at the coffee shop, she set off for the island in the grayish light that accompanied the fog in the pre-dawn chill. Traffic on the lake loop road was light, too early for both tourists and commuters.

Teague's pickup was in the carport and no lights were on in his apartment. Shea parked her car beside his truck, then fumbled in the dark for the boathouse key.

"You're up early." Teague's voice startled her. He loomed out of the mist like the villain in a horror movie.

She jumped, one hand at her throat. "Don't sneak up on me like that! I nearly had a heart attack."

"You didn't sleep any better than I did." It wasn't a question. He knew.

Shea's cheeks burned. "No," she admitted.

"Want to come up for a cup of coffee?"

The two of them upstairs in Teague's cozy little apartment, insulated from the world by a blanket of fog? Her heart cartwheeled a time or two as she considered the possibilities. "No thanks. I already had breakfast."

"It's only a little after five," Teague said. "No one's up yet on the island."

"I know."

He shot her a puzzled look. "If you didn't come to see me or one of the Raineys, then why *are* you here?"

"You'll think I'm crazy." If he didn't already.

"You're going to visit the old cabin," he said.

"How did you guess?"

"I noticed how agitated you were yesterday when we were with Mikey and before that, the time we took the walk along the shore. The closer we got to the cabin, the more you dragged your feet."

She shivered. "Agitated isn't quite the right word. Try scared. Or petrified. I admit my fear was irrational, but it was, nonetheless, an incredibly powerful emotion."

"So why go back? What are you trying to prove?"

"That I'm not a coward, I guess." She took a deep breath. "I've given this a lot of thought. My theory, the only one that makes sense to me, is that Kirsten had a bad experience there, perhaps saw something that frightened her. I can't prove it, but I believe I was experiencing her emotions, not my own."

"Okay, just for the sake of argument, let's say it was Kirsten's fear you felt. Why would she be afraid of the cabin? She used to spend hours down there sorting and identifying rocks."

Shea sighed. "I don't know. But if it's not her terror, then what's going on? I certainly don't have any firsthand associations to trigger panic."

"At least none that you're conscious of."

"Meaning?"

"Meaning you could have deeply buried memories of a similar spot. Did you ever get lost in the woods when you were a child?"

"No. Besides, the woods in Ohio don't look like the forests here."

He leaned against the hood of his pickup. "Okay, so maybe we're on the wrong track," he said. He thumped his forehead with the heel of his hand. "Wait a minute. Didn't you tell me you'd read about the Rainey massacre?"

"Yes," she admitted.

"Then maybe that's it."

"What's it?"

"The cabin's where all those people were butchered. If you're as sensitive to the atmosphere as I suspect, it may be the psychic pollution left in the wake of the massacre that's affecting you, and nothing to do with Kirsten at all."

Shea could tell he was pleased with his new theory. And though she had to admit it made sense—supposing one accepted the existence of psychic pollution—she still wasn't a hundred percent convinced. For one thing, Teague's theory didn't explain all those other flashes she'd had, like the one on the stairs in the Rainey house.

"If so, then there's nothing to worry about, and the sooner I face my irrational fear, the better. I'm going to the cabin."

"But it's dark and foggy." His objections made sense, but Shea had a feeling that if she didn't face her fears now, she might never work up enough courage again.

"The sun will be up soon, and the fog won't last long. It never does."

The mist was thinner right on the water than it had been along the shore, for which Teague was grateful. He'd had visions of them missing the island altogether in a pea-souper, then wasting half the morning and a tank of gas trying to get their bearings. But their trip across was uneventful. No one was around this early, not even the mallards that nested along the unpopulated end of Crescent Lake.

He tied the boat to the mooring at the end of the dock, then leaped onto the silvered boards with a hollow *thunk* that sounded preternaturally loud in the early-morning hush. He stretched out a hand to help Shea. Her fingers were icy. She stepped onto the dock with a muttered "Thanks." Huddling in her sweatshirt, she cocked her head to one side as if she were listening to the water lapping onto the pilings. "I hope we didn't wake the Griffins." She nodded toward the boathouse apartment.

"No lights," he said.

"What's the quickest, most direct route to the cabin?" She couldn't quite disguise the tremor in her voice.

"You don't have to do this, you know."

"Yes. I do." Scared spitless, but stubborn as ever.

"Straight across the island is the shortest route, but it would probably be faster to follow the shoreline than to stumble through the underbrush in the dark." And the fog, which was growing thicker by the minute. Mist cloaked the boathouse, distorting its outline.

Shea gave herself a shake. "If we're going, let's get on with it."

The shoreline was steep and rugged, lacking the occasional beaches and gentler slopes of the southern shore. Though the heavy undergrowth provided good handholds, they were soon wet to the skin. Every time they brushed against the lush foliage, they were showered by a misting of fine dew drops.

Once she slid down a steep incline and nearly landed in the lake. She caught herself just in time, grabbing a young pine seedling that thrust up at an angle from the rocky soil of the cliff.

As they circled around to the western shore, there was a reappearance of the ledges so common on the southern edge. This made walking marginally easier. The rocks were slippery, though nowhere near as treacherous as the wet grass and pine needles had been.

"We're almost there," Shea said suddenly. "I feel it."

All Teague felt was the chill of his wet clothes, but the murmur of the spring told him she was right. "We can still turn around."

She wanted to, he could tell. But she forced herself

forward until she stood at the very edge of the alder thicket. She poised there, listening. "Do you hear that?"

"What? The stream?"

"No, that thrumming sound."

He listened intently. No thrumming sound. Just water whispering over the weathered granite of the streambed and birds twittering in the trees.

Suddenly she gave a nervous laugh.

"What's the joke?"

"The thrumming. I figured out what it was . . . nothing more sinister than my own heartbeat. Sorry, Teague. I'm acting like an idiot. What is there to be frightened of, anyway? What's the worst that can happen? So I experience the memory of whatever traumatic event inspired Kirsten's terror. Big deal. Memory's the operative word here."

"Are you trying to convince me or yourself?"

"Myself. And it's not working." She took a deep breath. "The cabin's just beyond the trees, isn't it?"

"Yes." And he didn't know if her apprehension was contagious or what, but suddenly he wasn't any more anxious than she was to penetrate the leafy barrier.

The wind shifted subtly, stirring the mist in coiling currents. The sky had lightened. To the east, where the morning sun now blazed behind a blanket of vapor, the fog was so white, it made his eyes ache. It would be a fine day once the shrouding haze burned off, but right now the alder thicket was dark and dank. Wisps of mist moved sinuously among the trees, muffling sounds and intensifying odors. He sniffed pine, leaf mold, catnip, and, underneath it all, something else. Something unpleasant. Something that made the hairs stand up along his forearms.

"Kirsten?" Shea whispered.

Teague frowned. "Maybe this wasn't such a good idea."

"I've come this far. . . ." Taking a deep breath, she plunged into the thicket.

He was right behind her. Their noisy progress startled a covey of nesting birds that took off with a wild whirring of wings accompanied by shrill, frightened chittering.

"Be still, my heart," she said grimly.

Another step or two brought them into a tiny clearing almost entirely filled by the small, dilapidated cabin, its shake roof covered with moss, its door gaping open, as if surprised at their intrusion.

Teague grabbed Shea's arm in a restraining grasp. "Don't go in. The floor's probably rotten."

Shea shuddered. "I wouldn't dream of it. Rotten floorboards aside, like I told you before, I'm the poster kid for claustrophobia."

He peeked inside, but little was visible in the darkness beyond the doorway, curtained by cobwebs.

"I smell something dead." Her voice shook.

He nodded grimly. The stench of putrefying flesh was unmistakable. "Some animal must have plunged through those rotten floorboards and died in there."

"Poor thing." Shea shuddered again. "Maybe I caught a whiff of that smell the other times I came this way. Maybe that's what frightened me."

"Probably. Your subconscious made the connection even though the odor wasn't strong enough to alert your conscious mind." Braving the spiderwebs, he stuck his head in the door and took a deep breath. Unpleasant for sure. Dust, mold, and dampness. But the stench of death was definitely weaker. "Odd," he said. "We guessed wrong. The smell isn't from inside the cabin. Let's check around back."

Shea went one way and Teague the other, hugging the rough log walls and ducking to avoid the encroaching tree branches.

Once he rounded the corner, the smell was strong enough to gag him. Holding his breath, he inched forward through a bramble patch.

He cut his hand on a thorny cane when Shea let out a shriek so sharp, it shaved half a decade off his life span. A flock of crows, what seemed like dozens of them, flew up in a flurry of shiny black wings, several fluttering around his head like the crazed birds in Alfred Hitchcock's classic thriller. The din was incredible. For endless seconds the world was reduced to a whirling vortex of black feathers and a raucous cawing so loud, he felt as if his eardrums were about to burst.

Shea batted at the demonic birds, screaming hysterically. For a few heartstopping seconds she actually believed the big birds were launching a malevolent attack. Then reason reasserted itself, and she realized they were simply confused by her intrusion.

"Shea! Are you all right?" Teague called. He stared at her across the ten feet or so that separated them, looking as unnerved as she felt.

"I'm fine. Sorry I screamed. The birds startled me."

Two of the more brazen crows perched in a nearby tree. Staring.

Shea shivered, even though she soon realized she wasn't the focus of their rapt attention. The birds were fascinated with something that lay hidden between her and Teague, something just beyond her line of sight, something rankly putrescent.

"Teague?" She met his gaze and saw raw horror mirrored on his face.

"Don't look," he said.

She didn't have to. Her imagination had already supplied all the details. "Is it . . ."

Teague nodded, looking tired. "We just solved the mystery of the missing dog."

NINE

The sun burned through the fog, highlighting the gruesome details of the disturbed grave. Teague averted his eyes and circled the corpse to reach Shea. Pulling her close to his side, he urged her away from the grisly remains. She trembled violently. "Let's get out of here," he said.

"But shouldn't we tell someone? The sheriff maybe?"

"First priority is to get you out of those wet clothes and into a warm bath." She was in shock, he thought. Hell, he didn't feel exactly normal himself.

"Mikey's dog didn't die of natural causes."

"We don't know that for sure. Don't jump to conclusions," he said, even though he was certain she was right. "I'll alert the proper authorities and let them deal with it."

She stiffened and pulled away. "Not from the house! Mikey . . ."

He stroked her cheek, wanting to comfort her but not sure quite how. "From my place."

Clinging to each other, they retraced their path around the island. Shea didn't speak again until they reached the dock. As Teague readied the boat, she stared back over her shoulder. "What if Cynthia's return hadn't interrupted our visit to the cabin yesterday? I keep thinking about that. What if Mikey had run ahead and discovered Beelzebub's body herself?" She turned to face him, her eyes wide and glassy at the imagined horror.

Teague gathered her close. "Don't worry about what didn't happen." She was shivering uncontrollably. She needed to change into dry clothes.

"Do they perform autopsies on dogs?" she asked.

"Autopsies? Why?"

"Don't you want to know what killed Beelzebub?" she demanded.

He shrugged. "Dead is dead."

"Yes, but if we knew *what* killed him, we might be able to figure out *who* killed him. Think about it. If he was poisoned—"

"Like Jack, you mean?"

"What if someone used Beelzebub as a test subject to see how well the hemlock worked?"

Teague's gut twisted. "Let's go." What the hell had he involved her in?

Teague ushered Shea into his apartment. "Have a seat," he said, waving her toward the sofa.

"No, I'm covered with mud." In point of fact, only her shoes were mud-caked, as were his own. "A kitchen chair is fine."

"Why don't you go soak in a hot tub while I contact the sheriff?"

She nodded. "I can't seem to get warm."

He hunted up a box of odds and ends of Kirsten's old clothes he'd never been able to part with. "You'll probably find something in here to fit you."

"Kirsten's?"

"Just some stuff she left behind when she moved back to the island." To her death. A wave of guilt washed over him, so strong it threatened to erode his composure. If only he hadn't lost his temper . . .

Shea took the box and retreated to the bathroom, leaving him alone with his thoughts. This time he wouldn't make the same mistake. This time he'd control his temper. This time he'd keep her safe.

He called the sheriff, told him about finding Beelzebub, and explained the questionable circumstances surrounding the dog's death. Jim Carlton promised to send a deputy out to the island to collect the remains for testing. Dr. Zeller, a local vet, would do the autopsy.

"Oh, and before I forget," the sheriff said, "I finally tracked down a retired nurse who worked at the clinic where Kirsten was born. She's on vacation, but I left a message for her to call me when she gets home."

Next he called Cynthia at the hospital to let her know about their grisly discovery. She promised to explain everything to Kevin and make sure he kept Mikey out of the deputy's way.

Then finally he called his foreman. No point trying to work on Massacre Island today. He told Nick to take the crew out to get a head start on the greens renovation at the Crescent Lake Country Club instead.

❖━━━━━❖

When Teague came back into the living area after his own shower to see if Shea wanted some coffee, he found her asleep, curled up on one end of the sofa. He tucked the soft folds of a blanket around her, then wandered barefoot out to the end of the dock. He glanced up at the sound of a motor. Squinting into the sun, he made out the dark outline of the sheriff's cabin cruiser speeding away from Massacre Island. So they'd found the dog's remains. And perhaps Shea was right. Maybe the autopsy would tell them something. Like who was responsible for Beelzebub's death.

If he'd had to hazard a guess, he'd pick Ruth Griffin as his villainess of choice. She was just crazy enough. Maybe she'd convinced herself the black dog was the devil's henchman. Or maybe she'd whacked him one too many times with her broom, crushed his skull for tracking mud on the kitchen floor. Either way, though, she probably wasn't physically capable of hauling the dog all the way to the cabin to bury him. She'd have had to have help—most likely from one or both of the twins.

Shea woke to find Teague watching her, the expression on his face both intent and tender. She smiled. "I didn't mean to fall asleep."

"You'd had a shock."

Her smile faded. "We both did. What time is it?" She glanced at her wrist, then remembered she'd tossed her watch in the bathroom wastebasket. Sometime during their morning's adventure, she'd shattered the crystal, probably when she'd swung out wildly to protect herself from the flock of crows.

"Half-past noon. You hungry?"

She sat up. "Starved."

"Hungry enough to brave my cooking?"

Shea grinned. "Hungry enough to brave my *own* cooking."

He cocked an eyebrow. "Junior executives don't cook?"

"Not when they work twelve-hour days." Her grin turned sheepish. "And there's a Wendy's right on the way home."

Teague walked toward the kitchen alcove. "How about vegetable soup and a grilled cheese sandwich?"

She sat on one of the bar stools at the counter and watched him put together their lunch. Teague cooked with a neat efficiency Shea admired. The only dish she excelled at was lasagna, and even then she was likely to have as much sauce spattered across the stovetop or burned onto the bottom of her oven as ever made it into the lasagna itself. Cleanup inevitably took twice as long as the initial preparation.

They ate sitting side by side at the counter. "Why do you always do that?" she asked when she caught him staring at her for the second time in five minutes.

"I like the way you look when you're eating, as if every bite were an adventure."

She put her fork down. "But when you stare like that, I feel self-conscious. Like I have a milk mustache or something."

He stroked her upper lip with his forefinger.

She shivered in response.

"Nope," he said. "No full moon." He covered her hand, twining his fingers with hers. "I'm sorry if I make you feel uncomfortable, though."

Heat shot up her arm. She swiveled around to face

him, intending to say, "Thanks for lunch. I'd better be going now." Only when she saw his eyes, smoky with desire, she swallowed the words and brought her free hand up to caress his cheek.

His smile should have disarmed her. Instead, her heart rate tripled.

The angles of his face felt smooth and hard under her fingertips. The heat flowed up both arms, pooling in her breasts and between her legs. *I should leave*, she thought. But she didn't. "Kiss me."

When he licked his tongue inside her mouth, a jolt of raw desire rocked her like a surge of electricity. *Lightning strikes*, she thought, dizzy with wanting him.

Kissing Teague was good, no doubt about it. Kissing Teague was very, very good, but kissing Teague wasn't enough. Not this time. Shea made a yearning sound in her throat, not quite a moan, not quite a sigh. Something in between.

In response, he lifted her onto his lap so that she sat astride him. His gaze held hers.

She caught her lower lip between her teeth. Her body throbbed everywhere it made contact with his. *I want you*, she thought. *Touch me*.

Something sparked in his gaze as if he'd read her thoughts. He claimed her mouth again, kissing her deeply, passionately. The heat built, wave upon wave, until Shea felt as if she would burst into flames.

He nuzzled her throat, and she arched her neck, clinging to his shoulders. And when he slipped his hands under the hem of her borrowed T-shirt, unhooked her bra, and cupped her aching breasts, she shuddered with the pleasure of it, straining herself hard against his palms.

"Like that, do you?" he whispered.

"Oh, yes," she said, her breath catching in a gasp of delight as Teague brushed his thumbs across her nipples with a wickedly erotic friction.

He tugged the T-shirt over her head, slid the bra straps down her arms, then gazed at her in silence for a long moment. "You're beautiful," he said at last, his voice shaking slightly, "so damn beautiful."

Shea sank her nails into his shoulders and moaned his name when he lowered his mouth to her breast. Hooking her ankles around his waist, she pressed herself tightly against him. He shifted his attention to her other breast, and her pleasure spiraled to unbearable heights. She ached for him.

"Please." Frantic with need, she tugged the shirt over his head, then slid off his lap to fumble urgently with the zipper of his jeans. Her legs felt noodly, and her brain was Swiss cheese, empty spaces where reason and caution were supposed to be.

"Go easy," he said. "There's no hurry."

No hurry? Was he joking? If she didn't have him soon, she'd disintegrate.

With trembling hands, she helped him strip off the rest of her borrowed clothing. Then frustrated, desperate to feel him inside her, she attacked his zipper again, successfully this time, and dragged his jeans and shorts down to his knees. He kicked them off and reached for her, but she held him off. "No hurry," she reminded him.

His body was hard and ridged with muscles, so gorgeous her breath caught in her throat. She slid her hands, slowly and deliberately, across the planes of his chest, the bunched muscles of his arms. He quivered with tension.

She trailed her fingertips over his abdomen, leisurely counting his six-pack. Then she wrapped her fingers around his erection, sheathing him in her hands. "No hurry?" she asked softly as she squeezed and stroked.

"So maybe I overestimated my control." He grabbed her wrists. "Bedroom, dammit," he said with a groan.

"Bedroom?" She hadn't pegged him as the conventional type. "What's wrong with right here?"

Teague frowned with the effort to maintain control. "My Boy Scout training failed me this time. The condoms are in the nightstand."

He meant to take it slowly, to savor every second, but he hadn't counted on Shea. The instant he sat down on the edge of the bed to adjust the latex sheath, she wriggled up behind him and ran her nails lightly down his back.

He shuddered in reaction, then rolled over on her, pinning her to the bed. She wrapped her arms around his neck and pulled his mouth down hard on hers. She thrust her tongue into his mouth and he tasted her hot urgency.

He slid his hand between their bodies. She quivered at his touch, and when he began to stroke her, she shuddered and moaned and dug into his shoulders with her nails. "Now," she begged. "Now, Teague." And he slid inside, filling her with himself.

She clenched her muscles tight for a second, then with a moan surged up under him, rocking her body against his. Tension coiled tighter with each thrust of her hips. He held back as long as he could, but when she wrapped her legs around him, pulling him deeper into her velvety warmth, he gave himself up to the pleasure, rocking and pounding and surging with her until the feverish excitement exploded in an orgasm that ripped through his body like a seismic disturbance. Seconds later, she screamed her own release and melted into a boneless pool of contentment beneath him.

"Eight-point-three on the Richter scale," Shea said.

He lifted leaden lids to look at her and saw that her eyes were luminous, her mouth curved in a sweet smile.

He rolled over onto his side, cradling her against him spoon fashion. He ran one hand idly along her thigh, her taut abdomen, her soft, full breasts. *Hot satin*, he thought. *Hot satin over molten lava.* "My God, Kirsten," he mumbled into her shoulder. "I never felt anything close to that before. You're incredible."

Shea sat up abruptly. Teague lay there, smiling up at her, his eyes half shut. He looked so damn gorgeous, she could hardly stand it. The pain in her chest was unbearable; she could almost believe that hearts really did break in two. "Kirsten?" she whispered. She'd been a fool from the very beginning. She'd always known in her heart of hearts that it was Kirsten he loved, not Shea. Never Shea.

She stood, watching as the realization of his faux pas dawned on him. His face congealed into a mask of horrified contrition. Too little, too late.

"Shea. Shea, I'm sorry. It was a slip of the tongue. It didn't mean a thing. Honestly. I'm just so used to calling you Kirsten in front of the Raineys that I used the wrong name."

"Damn you, Teague Harris." If her voice was cold, her heart was colder, a lump of ice in her chest. She turned her back on him and walked from the room.

After gathering together her scattered clothes, Shea locked herself in the bathroom. She needed a shower, a long, hot shower.

She bawled herself dry in the first fifteen minutes, then spent the next fifteen minutes trying in vain to wash away her self-disgust.

Teague was a jerk, she was a fool, and the whole situation was a mess. Damn hormones.

By the time she got out of the shower, all the hot water was gone, her skin was shriveled, and she'd come to terms with the facts.

Fact one: She'd just hit the jackpot with a megaorgasm. Big deal. Happened every day. Okay, maybe not to her, but looking on the bright side, she'd have the memory of at least one mind-blowing sexual experience to comfort her in her old age.

Fact two: She was in love with Teague, but Teague was still in love with Kirsten. This fact was more painful to swallow, but it wasn't, she assured herself, a fatal dose. She would recover her perspective gradually over time and with distance. Especially with distance. Because even knowing it was Kirsten he saw when he looked at her, she knew that one hot glance from Teague's smoky gray eyes and she'd jump him like a trampoline. The sooner she left Liberty, the better. Tomorrow would be good; today might be better.

Fact three: Whoever had said it was better to have loved and lost than never to have loved at all was full of it. Big time.

She dressed in a rush, suddenly desperate to be gone. In her haste, she knocked over the key caddy, spilling its contents—mostly loose change, a couple of pairs of cufflinks, keys, and tie tacks.

She knelt to gather up the few items that had rolled onto the floor and discovered that one of them was a ring.

Not just any ring, either. Fear trickled an icy warning along her veins. An engagement ring. Kirsten's engagement ring, looking just as Kevin had described it, a pale aquamarine stone surrounded by a cluster of diamonds in a platinum setting.

She stared at it, momentarily paralyzed by dread. So where—and when—had Teague found this ring, which Kevin had said Kirsten never removed? Had Teague *killed* Kirsten? If not, then what was her ring doing in his apartment?

On the other hand, if he had killed her, why would he keep a piece of incriminating evidence lying around? That didn't make sense.

Shea held the ring to the light. Its sparkle reminded her of the crystal cluster in Kirsten's room on the island. She touched a facet with her forefinger, half expecting to experience the same rush she'd felt in her contact with the crystal, but nothing happened. "Kirsten?" she whispered, rolling the ring back and forth between her thumb and forefinger. The stones reflected the light, giving away no secrets.

She jumped when Teague hammered at the bathroom door. "Are you all right in there?"

For a moment she was speechless. Panic scrambled her brain and dried her mouth. Was he a murderer or not? She didn't have a clue. All she knew for certain was that she couldn't let him suspect what she'd discovered. She buried the ring under the pile of loose change, wincing at the rattle of the coins. Had he heard? Would he realize what she was doing?

"I'm okay," she answered. Her voice shook a little, but perhaps he'd put that down to her outraged sensibilities. Calling the woman you just made love with by your dead wife's name was a pretty major social gaffe.

"Then could you open the door? We need to talk." His voice was soft and urgent, his tone persuasive, but still Shea hesitated. How could she trust him? He'd always acted as if he were hiding something when they discussed Kirsten's disappearance. Maybe he hadn't killed her, but he obviously knew more about what had happened than he'd admitted.

"Did you hear me?" His fists banged out a staccato rhythm on the bathroom door.

She clicked the lock, turned the knob, then slowly pushed the door open. "I heard you." She shot him a nervous sideways glance. She had to get out of there. She needed to be alone to make sense of things.

"Dammit, Shea," he said, reaching out to take her by the shoulders. "Let me explain."

"Not now." She shied away, and his eyes went opaque with pain. She couldn't bear to look at them, so she shifted her gaze to her own clenched fists.

"I don't want you to go." His voice was a whisper, tender and pleading, and it cut her like a knife. But when he touched her face tentatively, she stiffened and he let his hand drop. "I made a mistake, Shea, a stupid slip of the tongue. I'm so very sorry. Believe me, I never meant to hurt you."

"Teague, I can't discuss this rationally right now. I need some time alone to put things in perspective." She risked a quick glance at his face, then wished she hadn't. He looked so wretched that she nearly relented, despite what she suspected.

"Shea." His voice was husky with suppressed emotion. "Before you go, I just want to say one thing." He took a deep breath.

She stared at him, her expression carefully neutral.

"I love you, Shea. Not Kirsten. You."

If only she could believe that. If only she could trust him. She edged toward the door, her heart pounding like a whole section of timpani players high on amphetamines.

Teague stepped in front of her, cutting off her escape route. "Please don't walk out on me, Shea." His face mirrored her own anguish, but she hardened her heart against him.

"You mean the way Kirsten walked out on you? What did you two quarrel about? What sent her running home to Daddy?" Her random shot found its target.

His face hardened. "That's none of your concern." The words themselves were spoken softly, but they still sent a ripple of alarm shivering down her spine. Dear God, *could* he be the killer?

The schoolhouse clock on the wall above the bookcase bonged out the hour. Two o'clock. So early. It seemed she'd been there a lifetime. Teague stared down at her, his expression unreadable. Her hands trembled. Her heart raced. Was Kirsten about to disappear again?

Fighting off a rising tide of panic, she ducked under his arm and dashed for the door, snatching up her purse as she went. Her heartbeat echoed so loudly in her ears, it nearly drowned out the sounds of pursuit. She was mere inches from freedom, with one hand actually grasping the doorknob, when he caught up with her.

A single violent tug loosened her grip on the knob

and brought her spinning around to face him. Both of them were breathing hard.

"Dammit, Shea. Don't look at me like that."

"Like what?"

"Like you're scared to death I'm going to hurt you."

"You *are* hurting me."

His mouth twisted in pain as if the circulation was being cut off to *his* hand. He loosened his grip, but he didn't release her wrist. "I'm sorry."

"You said that already."

"I don't want you to leave like this," he said.

"You said that too."

"Tell me what I haven't said then. Tell me the words I need to make you understand how much I love you."

His gaze searched her face and seemed to probe the corners of her mind. She tried not to think about the ring, about her suspicions. "There are no words," she said.

Abruptly, he dropped her wrist. "Then I guess there's nothing left to say but good-bye."

She couldn't put a name to his expression, but she felt bruised by its force. She left without another word.

TEN

By six, Shea was packed and ready to start hauling her gear out to the car. While she was debating with herself whether to leave a note for the Raineys at the desk or call tomorrow from a pay phone along the road, the telephone rang. *Teague*, she thought, and almost didn't answer it. But she couldn't stand to let it ring. Cautiously, she lifted the receiver.

"Kirsten?"

"Kevin?" Her heart did a little flip-flop of alarm. "What is it?"

"Dad's taken another turn for the worse."

"What happened?"

"Someone tried to smother him with a pillow."

"What? How is he?"

"Holding his own. Barely. A nurse walked in just in time to scare off the would-be murderer."

"She saw him then?"

"Not clearly. All she could swear to was that it was a big man in jeans and a dark hooded jacket."

Like the navy-blue one Teague had worn to the island this morning? But he couldn't have tried to kill Jack, could he? Teague admired Jack, loved him like a father—unless that relationship was as phony as their own false engagement. Her stomach rolled and she felt light-headed. All at once she realized Kevin had just asked her something. "What?"

"Can you stay with Mikey?"

"Where? The island?"

"Yes."

"Okay, I guess—"

"Good. Hurry." He hung up without even saying good-bye.

Shea stared at her luggage in defeat. It seemed she wasn't going to leave Liberty just yet.

"The girl's not just Jack's daughter," Sheriff Carlton told Teague. "According to the records from that Los Angeles fertility clinic, she's Kirsten's twin."

"But that's impossible. Different mothers. Different birthdays."

"Wrong." The sheriff handed him the report. "When Elizabeth Rainey discovered she was unable to have children, the doctors suggested that she and her husband use a surrogate mother to carry their child."

"Shea's mother."

The sheriff nodded. "Christine Miller, a young nursing student who agreed to be artificially inseminated with Jack's sperm and carry their child to term in return for her tuition and expenses."

"Only the child turned out to be twins."

"Right. Knowledge Miss Miller never shared with the

Raineys. According to the nurse who worked at the clinic back then, the girl was tortured with guilt at the thought of parting with her child. So when she discovered there were two children, she saw it as God's way of evening things out, and she decided to keep the second child."

"But the birthdates are different. Kirsten was born in June, Shea in July."

"Both babies were born on June fifth." The sheriff tossed him a fax of the birth certificates. "The woman must have doctored her copy, hoping to bury the truth. What concerns me, though . . . is the fact that someone else has been investigating the clinic."

"Who?"

"A PI out of Boise who refuses to divulge the name of his client."

"So someone else knows who Shea really is."

"It could be Jack," the sheriff said.

"Or it could be someone with reason to know Shea isn't Kirsten. Kirsten was murdered, Sheriff. I'm sure of it. And now Shea may be in danger too."

Shea and Mikey were alone in the house on Massacre Island. Kevin had left for the hospital soon after she'd arrived, and now, at ten-thirty, with Mikey asleep upstairs, Shea found herself wandering from door to door, checking and rechecking the locks. She paused near the sliding glass doors in the dining room, peering out at the blackness beyond the spotlit pool.

Something moved out there, where trees and bushes edged the deck. Flipping on the security lights, she stared intently at the spot where she'd seen the flicker of movement, but all was still.

The moon was up, gibbous, a week or more away from being full. Its cool light flooded the yard, illuminating the area around the house. Shadows stretched inky fingers toward the house, ebony on silver, jet on gray, their tortured shapes creating monsters from the mundane. A decorative boulder changed into a prehistoric beast lying in wait, and the espaliered fruit trees along the fence became the skeletal remains of crucified martyrs. Shea stared until her eyes watered, but nothing moved.

"So much for my lurid imagination," she muttered, and was about to turn away when she caught another glimpse of movement from the corner of her eye. Her heart made a leap for her throat, and her breath came in painful gasps. She concentrated so fiercely on the spot, she felt as if her eyes would burst from the strain.

Then from the midst of a clump of peonies at the far end of the planting bed waddled the slightly ridiculous figure of a skunk. Cursing herself for being a paranoid idiot, Shea turned away from the doors.

The phone rang, jarringly loud in the silent house. She slipped into the kitchen and grabbed the extension. "Hello?"

"Shea? I just got back from the lodge. They said you checked out this afternoon. What are you doing on the island?" Teague. She should have known.

"I'm staying here."

"Alone?"

"No, of course not." It wasn't a lie. Ruth and Hal Griffin were attending an all-night prayer vigil for Jack at the Tabernacle of the Blessed and Kevin and Cynthia were at the hospital, but Glory was in the Griffin apartment, nursing a headache, and Mikey was right upstairs.

"You're lying. I can hear it in your voice. Shea, listen. You may be in danger. I want you to lock yourself in and sit tight. I'll be right over."

"No!"

"Shea, you've got to trust me."

"The way Kirsten trusted you?"

She heard a sharp intake of breath on his end of the connection. "Shea—"

"I found her engagement ring in your bathroom."

"What?"

"You know, the ring she never took off. The ring she was wearing the day she disappeared."

"I had nothing to do with her disappearance."

"Then how did the ring end up in your apartment?"

"Things have been turning up ever since the break-in, a barrette, her favorite earrings."

"You're suggesting someone planted evidence in your apartment to frame you for Kirsten's murder? How could that someone know I'd find the ring?"

"I doubt he intended to frame me. The arrogant son of a bitch was just rubbing my nose in the fact that the real Kirsten was dead."

His story had a certain twisted plausibility. She could almost believe it. Almost.

"What really happened during that argument with Kirsten? Did you get a little carried away? Hit her a little too hard?"

"Oh, God. We need to talk."

That didn't sound like a denial.

"We are talking."

"Face-to-face."

"Stay away from me, Teague. I don't trust you."

"But I need to explain."

"What? How you killed your wife? What happened? Did she tell you the baby wasn't yours?"

"Dammit, I loved Kirsten. And believe it or not, I love you."

"Stay away from me," she repeated, and hung up.

No sooner had she replaced the receiver than the phone rang again.

Shea stared at the telephone as if it were a rattler about to strike. Maybe if she just let it ring, he'd get the hint. Or not, she thought as the ringing continued unabated. On ring fifteen, she snatched up the receiver. "Dammit, Teague! I don't want to talk to you!"

"Kirsten?"

Kevin, not Teague. "Sorry about that. I thought . . . Never mind. How's Daddy?"

"Hanging in there."

"Could I talk to Cynthia for a minute?" she asked.

"Sorry. She just slipped down the hall in search of a coffee machine. Was it important?"

"No, not really. Tell her I'm thinking of her, okay?"

"How are you doing?" Kevin asked.

"Fine."

"I take it Teague tracked you down."

She made a noncommittal sound.

"What did he have to say?"

"Nothing I wanted to hear." Her flat tone put an end to that line of questioning. "The only other excitement was when I thought I saw something moving in the bushes earlier."

"Oh, yeah?" She could almost see his ears perking up.

"Turned out to be a skunk."

Kevin chuckled. "I'll call if there's any change in

Dad's condition," he promised. "Keep the doors locked and watch out for skunks. Both the human and animal varieties."

After he hung up, she tried to watch TV but couldn't concentrate. After channel surfing for twenty minutes, she finally gave up and went upstairs for what was probably the shortest shower in history.

The whole time the water was running, she kept remembering the famous scene from *Psycho*. The fact that this shower stall had a very solid frosted-glass door instead of a flimsy plastic curtain didn't put her mind at rest.

Following her quick scrubdown, she changed into her nightie, checking once more on Mikey before moving next door to Kirsten's room. Kevin had left it unlocked for her use. She'd brought the portable phone from downstairs, just in case. Absentmindedly, she moved things aside to make room on the bedside table.

She should have been more careful. The instant her fingers touched the jagged surfaces of the aquamarine crystal cluster, a surge passed through her body. Her hand tightened convulsively. The razor-sharp edges bit into her hand. She watched in horrified disbelief as her blood filled the crevices of the crystal. A humming filled her ears, reverberating throughout her body. She shook uncontrollably, as if seized with palsy. *The secret's in the stone.* It was her last conscious thought before Kirsten's memories took control.

She was sitting on a flat-topped boulder at the edge of the clearing in front of the old cabin waiting for Teague. The odd part was, Teague was never late.

Maybe she'd misunderstood his note. She dug a folded paper from the pocket of her shorts. Five o'clock, his note said. Five o'clock at the old cabin.

When she'd found it stuffed under her bedroom door, her first thought was that Teague had relented and the wedding was back on. Yes, okay, she'd lied, but he didn't have to make a federal case out of it, did he?

The weather was unusually hot and muggy, the sky a sullen, brassy color. Perspiration dampened her bangs and made her shirt cling wetly to her back. At this rate, she was going to need another shower before dinner.

Shifting position, Kirsten brushed impatiently at the cloud of persistent gnats dive-bombing her face. What was keeping Teague?

She stood up with a shrug. As long as she was there, she might as well have another look at the newest addition to her collection. It sat on the shelf inside next to her Gem State Rockhound's Bible. *She hauled both book and rock back outside, where the light was better.*

Kirsten held the clump of blue-green crystals so that they'd catch the soft light filtering down through the leaves. As she turned the sample this way and that, its facets glittered aqua fire like sunlight sparkling off tropical seas.

It was a gorgeous specimen with long, well-defined crystals, doubly special because it had been a birthday present from Kevin. According to the Rockhound's Bible, *it was a blue-green form of beryl known as aquamarine—just like the central stone of her engagement ring.*

A breeze stirred through the thicket, rich with the scent of humus. Thunder growled an ominous threat, and lightning flashed over the mountains to the west, where thunderheads were building fast.

She drummed her fingers impatiently on the spine of the

book. It was getting late, and it looked as if it would rain. Where was Teague, anyway? She scanned the clearing, a slight frown knitting her brow. She was alone.

A lone crow flew over, rasping out what sounded like an insult. Or the punch line of a dirty joke. Kirsten checked her watch. Five more minutes. She'd give Mr. Teague Harris five more minutes, then she really had to go. If he wanted to kiss and make up, then he could damned well be on time.

Behind her a twig snapped with a sharp crack that sounded as loud as a rifle shot in the late-afternoon hush. Kirsten whirled around, but no one was there. "Teague?" She smiled. "Wolfman, is that you?" She peered into the greenery.

No answer. No Teague. No nothing. Must be an animal, she told herself.

She settled back down on the flat rock. Laying the Rockhound's Bible aside, she picked up the crystal cluster once again. The flickering sunlight caught the crystalline facets in a mesmerizing dazzle. The stone seemed to burn with an interior fire like a sliver off a hot blue star.

A tiny rustle of sound from behind alerted her. Her fingers tightened involuntarily, and she felt a sharp pain where the crystal sliced into her hand. Blood flowed warmly, smearing the surfaces of the rock. Then a shadow fell between her and the sun. "Teague?"

She started to turn, but before she was halfway around, something slammed into the back of her head with tremendous force. Her brain exploded in pain, terrible pain. And then there was nothing.

The telephone rang insistently. Shea fought her way back to consciousness through a fuzzy dream state. Her entire body felt inordinately heavy, as if she were pulling about five Gs, but her eyelids were leaden. She pried them open, then belatedly became aware of the sharp pain slicing across the fingers of her right hand.

Staring down in surprise, she discovered she had cut herself on the edges of the crystal cluster she was still clutching. The flow had already begun to clot, though blood was still welling up in fat drops along the two parallel lines that slashed diagonally across her fingers.

She dropped the crystal, wrapped her hand in the tail of her nightie, then awkwardly, using her left hand, answered the phone. "Hello?"

"Were you asleep?" Kevin asked.

Not the toughest question in the world, but she wasn't sure she knew the answer to it. Had the whole experience been nothing more than a particularly vivid dream? Or had she just relived another of Kirsten's memories? *Were you asleep?* Darned if she knew.

"Why are you calling again so soon? Is something wrong?" Besides the fact that she might be losing her mind.

"Soon? It's been hours since I called you."

Shea grabbed the portable alarm clock from the bedside table. Four minutes past three. So she must have fallen asleep on Kirsten's bed. And dreamed Kirsten's nightmare. "Sorry if I seem a little groggy, Kevin. I'm never at my best in the wee hours."

"Who is? Mom just crashed a little while ago. I guess she felt she could relax now that there are two deputies posted outside Dad's door."

She frowned. "If Daddy's all right, then why did you call?"

"Just checking in. Sweet dreams." He hung up while Shea was still pondering the irony of his final words.

After washing her cuts, she sprayed them with antiseptic and covered them with a gauze pad secured by half a roll of adhesive tape. The lacerations were fairly superficial, though the ones on her index finger were still oozing blood. She flexed her hand experimentally. Not bad. A little sore, but usable.

Shea returned to Kirsten's bedroom, more disturbed by her nightmare than by a few cuts. Had it been a nightmare? she asked herself. Or another of Kirsten's memories? And if it *had* been a memory—as she strongly suspected it was—what had triggered it? The room? The stone? Or was Kirsten herself trying to warn her of some present danger?

"Kirsten? Are you there?" She peered at herself in the cheval glass, searching her features for some hint of an alien presence, but she looked pretty much the way she always looked—discounting the circles under her eyes. "Who killed you, Kirsten? Who was it?"

Shea's eyes grew round as the truth hit her with the force of a sledgehammer blow. "You don't know," she whispered. "You never saw who hit you, did you?"

A wave of pain and frustration flooded her. Kirsten's pain. Kirsten's frustration. *Please. I need your strength. Together we can find the truth.* The words swirled through her head like a handful of confetti in a cold wind.

She didn't have a clue as to who had killed Kirsten, but the compulsion to visit the scene of the crime was suddenly overwhelming. "This is insane," she told herself out loud. "I'm listening to voices in my head." But she got dressed, anyway, then called Glory to baby-sit Mikey. "I've got to go out for a while and I don't want to leave her alone. How's your headache?"

"Headache?" Glory echoed. She evidently wasn't

tracking too well. Most people didn't when first awakened from a sound sleep.

"Sorry about waking you, but it couldn't be helped. How about it? Will you come stay with Mikey for a while?"

"Be right there," Glory said.

Shea hung up, then made a slow, sweeping survey of the room. The crystal cluster glittered in the glow of the bedside lamp.

Take it. The words echoed in her head. *The crystal's the connection.*

Not questioning the source of her knowledge, Shea stuffed the heavy aquamarine deep into one of the big pockets of her sweatshirt. Now what else did she need?

A flashlight. Ruth keeps them in a drawer in the kitchen. Once again Shea accepted the knowledge as a gift.

Quietly, she slipped downstairs and, without thinking about it, opened the right drawer on the first try. The flashlights were lined up inside, smallest to largest, just as she had pictured them. Shea chose the biggest one, reasoning that it could double as a weapon in a pinch.

She drummed her fingertips on the countertop. What else did she need?

A shovel. The words popped into her head unbidden.

A shovel? "Am I going to be digging then?" she whispered, but there was no answer. "Okay, a shovel it is."

Most of the tools were stored in the shed near the Griffins' house, but a few gardening implements were kept in the crawlspace under the deck.

She shivered as she stepped out the kitchen door into the cool, damp night. The customary scent of pine was overlaid by the heavy, almost sickeningly sweet odor of the alyssum in the planter edging the deck. The night was still but full of sounds—a frog chorus down by the lake, the periodic crackle of moths electrocuting themselves in the bug zapper, the distant rumble of a train passing through Liberty.

She left the deck for the shadows of the lawn, moving cautiously. The wet grass quickly soaked her shoes, and a full squadron of mosquitoes buzzed her ears in preparation for a major offensive. She waved them away impatiently, wishing she'd had the foresight to spray herself with insect repellent.

Something rustled in the deep shadows near the edge of the shrubbery bed. She froze, straining her ears in the darkness.

Nothing.

Probably just the skunk she'd seen earlier, she told herself, but couldn't shake the unnerving certainty that someone or something was watching her from the cover of darkness.

When an owl glided past on silent wings, hooting softly, she started violently, turning to follow its hushed progress. As she did, she noticed her own telltale tracks in the dew-soaked grass. If anyone was shadowing her, she was certainly making the job easy for him or her. She shivered again, this time not with the cold.

She doused her light and made a dash for the far side of the pool, feeling less vulnerable once she had gained the relative safety of a position deep in the inky shadows near the base of the deck. Her eyes and ears alert for any signs of pursuit, Shea crouched in the darkness long enough to allow her panicked respiratory system to resume normal operations. Then she flicked the light back on, training its beam on the bolt that secured the door to the space under the deck.

The mechanism was stiff with rust. Evidently no one had used it in a while. She fought the stubborn metal in an agitated silence, anxiety pushing her to hurry, hurry. The bolt broke free with a crack. She slid it to the right to release the catch, then shoved the door open.

Shea shone the flashlight into the narrow space under the deck. The plastic toolbox was there, just as Kirsten had remembered, the bright blue of its surface nearly obscured by a thick layer of dust. Shea dragged it out and opened it.

Once again something rustled in the bushes. Shea froze, holding her breath and listening intently, but all she heard were the normal night sounds. Insects. The subdued mutter of a boat motor echoing across the lake.

Dammit. She was as jittery as a grasshopper in a henhouse.

Digging through the box, she found a spade and, as an afterthought, added a pair of heavy gardening gloves to her equipment. Then she put the box back where she'd found it and closed the door in the lattice.

Teague watched Shea's shadowy figure dart around the end of the pool and disappear behind the deck. What the hell was she up to? He'd told her to sit tight, but he might have known she wouldn't. Dammit, he'd lost her!

No, there she was, following the bobbing circle of her flashlight up the path that led back across the island. Where the hell was she going?

Shea was thankful for the flashlight. It was pitch dark under the trees. No moonlight penetrated the heavy canopy of old-growth timber. Every few yards or so she surprised another small nocturnal creature, its bewildered eyes reflecting an eerie luminescent red in the glare of the powerful flashlight. No skunks or porcupines, though, for which she was grateful.

She made good time up the main path, but when she paused at the crest of the trail to catch her breath, she saw a flicker of movement on the path behind her. Quickly she switched off her light and ducked behind a patch of huckleberry bushes. She lay prone, hardly daring to move, all her attention trained on the path.

She had almost convinced herself that she was worrying about nothing when a large figure detached itself from the shadows and came racing up the trail. Teague Harris.

Cold sweat broke out across her forehead as she recognized his familiar form. Her stomach gave a warning heave, then she tasted bile.

He loped past her position, swearing under his breath. He must have been following her light, then panicked when it disappeared.

And that meant she had five minutes, tops. As soon as he realized she wasn't up ahead, the first thing he would do was backtrack to the spot where he'd lost her. This spot. Therefore, the sensible thing to do was to put as much ground as possible between herself and this clump of huckleberry bushes.

She fled down the path, back the way she had come. Did he know where she was headed? Probably not, she reasoned. Otherwise he wouldn't have acted so upset at losing her.

Fortunately, there was more than one way to approach the old cabin site. Rather than take the path through the woods, she could follow the shore. It would be a tricky journey in the dark, but she didn't dare use the flashlight again; the glow would betray her whereabouts and she had to avoid Teague at all costs.

Just trying to negotiate the slippery path without taking a serious spill took so much concentration, she had little attention to spare for worrying. It wasn't until she reached the scrubby growth along the perimeter of the alder thicket that the familiar dread hit her full force, curdling her stomach like the sudden onset of food poisoning.

She sniffed the air cautiously. No trace of putrescence remained, yet the place was still steeped in a brooding, ominous atmosphere. If a vampire had suddenly appeared to requisition a couple pints of her Type A positive, she wouldn't have been a bit surprised.

"What the hell brought you out here, McKenzie?" The sound of her own voice sent shivers running down her spine.

Why *had* she come all this way in the dark? Shea wasn't quite sure. Because of a bad dream? Or because a dead woman had planted the suggestion in her head?

She circled the copse cautiously until she stumbled across the entrance to a mazelike path she hadn't realized existed, then slipped soundlessly down it, following the comforting cone of light blazing from the end of her powerful flashlight.

The cabin was just as forlorn and depressing as she remembered from her previous visit. If anything, it was even less appealing in the dark. She set the flashlight down on a rock—the same rock where Kirsten had been sitting in her dream—and pulled on the gardening gloves. Shuddering, she remembered the cobwebs curtaining the cabin's doorway.

What do you think you're doing? she asked herself. Dread twisted her gut. *You aren't really planning to venture inside that filthy hovel, are you?*

Evidently she was, because the next thing she knew, she was ducking her head to avoid hanging spiderwebs and brandishing spade and flashlight as if they were weapons, not tools.

It stank inside, not of decayed flesh, but of dust and age and the stale popcorn odor of mice.

She tested the floorboards carefully, but they felt solid despite their seeming state of decrepitude. Once inside, she used the spade to knock away heavy ropes of cobwebs, then explored the interior methodically. It didn't take long. Even the shelves were gone now. Aside from years of accumulated filth, the room was empty.

So what was the big secret? Why had both Kirsten and Beelzebub been attacked there?

Hold on, her skeptical side cautioned. *You don't know for a fact that either one was ambushed here. Beelzebub could have been killed anywhere on the island before being buried here, and you don't know what happened to Kirsten.*

But she did know. The certainty had been growing ever since she woke up. Her nightmare had been a rerun of Kirsten's final memories. Kirsten hadn't run away, and she certainly hadn't been kidnapped. Someone had bashed her over the head as she sat outside in the sunshine waiting for Teague. Shea knew it as surely as she knew her own name.

What she didn't know was what had happened to the body. Was Kirsten in a watery resting place at the bottom of Crescent Lake? Or had she met Beelzebub's fate, buried in a shallow grave somewhere in the clearing?

Bright rodent eyes peered mockingly at her from the corner. Shea, who loathed mice, spun around in near panic, heading for the door. But as she started to bolt, the floor beneath her feet gave a warning creak that halted her in her tracks.

Her heart thumping in her ears, she angled the beam of the flashlight down, then sighed in relief to discover that she wasn't poised on a weak floorboard that was about to send her plunging down into the earth-walled cellar. What she'd discovered instead was a trapdoor.

She moved aside to study it. The door was a rough square that lay flush with the rest of the floor. A notch cut in one end obviously served as the handle.

Shea swore fluently under her breath as she considered her alternatives. She had faced up to the challenge of the thicket at night; she'd even drummed up the requisite courage to brave the cabin's interior, but she was damned if she was going to climb willingly into some dark, damp hole in the ground. "Forget it!" she muttered, but nevertheless proceeded to raise the trapdoor, grunting with the effort. The door was heavier than it looked.

Her nose twitched at the rush of damp air. The cellar smelled like worms and mold and dirt. She trained her flashlight into the opening, but all she could see was a small area of the packed-earth floor. A crude homemade ladder led down into the shadows below. Shea moved the light around, trying to make out details. There were none. Just more dirt floor. If she were going to do a thorough search, she would have to venture down the ladder.

You know how much you hate small, enclosed places, warned the coward inside.

On the other hand, since she'd come this far . . .

She started down the ladder, telling herself it really wasn't that bad. One foot after another—that's all it took. Gritting her teeth, she descended into the darkness.

The spade she'd tucked under her arm shifted and she nearly lost her grip on the ladder. "Dammit!" She let the shovel drop. Trying to cling to the ladder and handle the flashlight at the same time was a sufficiently tricky juggling act.

No sooner had the thought passed through her mind than her right foot met emptiness. A broken rung. Caught off-balance, she fell the last few feet. She landed with a jarring thump that left her shaken, but not hurt. *And for my next stunt . . .* Shea giggled weakly. She was crazy. No doubt about it.

Overhead, the floorboards creaked. Quickly she switched her light off, but the darkness was not complete. Through the opening in the floor above, she watched the glow of the intruder's flashlight grow brighter.

"Shea? Are you down there?" The whisper chilled her blood.

Teague. Why did it have to be Teague? She blinked away from the sudden glare of his flashlight.

"Shea? Are you all right? What are you doing wandering around out here in the middle of the night? I told you to lock yourself in the house."

"Why are you on Massacre Island?" she challenged. His face was a goblin mask of light and shadow in the backwash of the flashlight.

"Trying to protect you," he said in the same raspy

voice she had grown to love. Only now it raised goose-flesh on her arms.

"Protect me from what?" Shea peered up at him beseechingly, wanting to hear an explanation she could accept as truth.

Teague stared at her in silence.

"Protect me from what?" she repeated.

"From me." A second, shadowy figure loomed up behind Teague. Shea heard a heavy *thunk*. Then Teague dropped his flashlight into the hole. It bounced against a rung and ricocheted off in a wide arc. An inauspicious tinkle of breaking glass marked its landing, and the scene was plunged into darkness. Shea took an instinctive step backward just as a body came hurtling down to land with a sickening thud at her feet.

"Kevin!" she screamed. "What are you doing?"

The sound of his chuckle floated eerily out of the darkness just before the trapdoor crashed closed.

"Kevin! Have you lost your mind? You can't leave us here!"

Kevin didn't argue with her. Apparently he had his own agenda. The hammering lasted ten minutes or so. And then there was silence.

Dear God, she realized, they were buried alive.

ELEVEN

The pounding dragged Teague back to full consciousness, each thump of Kevin's hammer like a blow to Teague's aching head. When silence descended at last and he could think again, he groped in the darkness for his flashlight, finding Shea's ankle instead.

She squealed in surprise, then turned her own flashlight full in his face.

He groaned, squinting against the glare.

"Sorry," she said, moving the light out of his eyes. "You scared me." Though her voice was breathy with the panic that surrounded her in a near-visible fog, she knelt beside him, putting concern for him ahead of her fears. "Lie still. You may have a concussion. Let me check your head." She tugged off her gloves and ran her hands over his skull.

"Ouch!" he protested when her fingers pressed a tender spot on the back of his head. "That hurts."

"The skin's not broken."

"Yeah, but what about the bone? What happened? I'm a little fuzzy on the details."

"Kevin bonked you over the head with the traditional blunt object, shoved you into the cellar, and nailed the trapdoor shut."

Teague swore. "He shoved you in too?" He squinted at her, trying hard to focus.

"No. I was dumb enough to climb down on my own," she said, disgust edging her words.

"Why?"

"I had another Kirsten episode this evening. I think this is where she died. I came here to look for some evidence that might tell me who killed her and why."

"I can tell you who. Kevin," he said, "though God knows why or how, for that matter. He was only twelve."

Shea sighed. "Doesn't matter now, anyway. We need to concentrate on escaping from this oversize tomb." She stuffed the flashlight into Teague's hands. "Here. Hold this."

"What are you doing?"

"I'm going to try to break out of this dungeon before my claustrophobia kicks in and/or you die of internal injuries. You look like hell."

He felt worse. "Kevin nailed the door shut, Shea."

"I know, but maybe the wood is rotten. Or maybe he doesn't pound nails any better than he drives cars." She mounted the ladder, then pressed one shoulder to the trapdoor. "Cross your fingers and pray for dry rot or termites." She hit the trapdoor with her shoulder. It didn't budge. "If at first and all that." She hit it again and groaned.

"Shea, quit before you hurt yourself."

"Too late." She stumbled back down the ladder, nursing a bruised shoulder.

He shot her an encouraging grin as she plopped down on the ground beside him. "Give me a few minutes to pull myself together and I'll try."

But his bravado didn't fool her for a second. He read fear in her eyes. "No, Teague, I don't think so. You're hurt. Hurt bad. Truth is, we're never going to get out of here, are we? Not alive, anyway." She huddled in her sweatshirt, hugging her knees. "And it's all my fault. You wouldn't be in this mess if you hadn't been worried about me. I'm sorry, Teague, sorry about that and sorry about distrusting you too."

"You might have been more disposed to give me the benefit of the doubt if I hadn't called you Kirsten."

"Your timing was unfortunate." She stared at her clenched hands, never once glancing at him.

"Shea, do you remember what else I said? I never felt anything close to that before. Not with Kirsten. Not with anyone but you. I may have confused the names, but not the women."

"I wish I could believe that."

"Believe it. I was crazy about Kirsten, but I don't think our marriage would have lasted. Neither one of us was mature enough to handle a long-term relationship."

"But mature enough to make a baby."

"There was no baby, Shea. Kirsten lied about being pregnant, lied to her father and to me."

Shea shot him a startled glance.

"When I found out, we fought about it. I insisted that she tell her father the truth. She refused. She wanted that stupid wedding more, I think, than she ever wanted me."

"Teague, I'm sorry."

"So am I. If I had discussed the matter like a rational human being instead of ranting like a madman, Kirsten never would have run home to Daddy. My temper drove her into harm's way."

She placed one hand on his forearm, a casual touch, but he felt the jolt of the contact clear to his toes. "Your feelings of guilt are blinding you to the truth. It didn't matter to Kevin whether Kirsten was on the island or not. He'd have killed her no matter where she was."

"But I made it easier for him." Ignoring the pain, he sat up, resting his back against the ladder.

"Kirsten made it easier for him. She was the one who was trying to manipulate everyone to get what she wanted. She was the one who stormed off when she didn't get her way." Shea pulled his hands into her own and gripped them tightly as if she were determined to squeeze some sense into him.

She still loved him, he realized with a relief so intense, he felt dizzy with it.

"Kirsten doesn't blame you, Teague. Don't you think I'd know it if she did?" She smiled. "And you know what else?"

"What?" It was hard to talk with your heart clogging your throat. Her smile was doing weird things to his breathing too.

"I love you, Teague Harris, and I'm not going to waste any more time being jealous of a dead woman." Shea pressed her sweet mouth to his, and the world dissolved around them.

For a brief moment he didn't feel the throb of his head or the pain in his legs, aware only of Shea and how much he loved her. Then she pulled away with a sigh, and their surroundings swam back into focus. The grimness of their situation hit him like a blow to the solar plexus.

"You've got to get out of here," he said.

She shot him a startled look. "*We've* got to get out of here, you mean."

"I'm not going anywhere, Shea. You were right. I am hurt bad. I'm pretty sure both legs are broken."

She studied him in silence as the sense of his words sank in. She looked stricken for a split second. Then she squared her jaw. "I'm not leaving you. Maybe we can reason with Kevin."

"How do you reason with a murderer? He killed Kirsten and now he's after you."

"But why? I'm no threat to him."

"Yes, you are, and I think he knows that."

"But—"

Teague outlined the information the sheriff's investigation had revealed. "You suspected all along that Jack was your father, didn't you? That's why you agreed to the charade in the first place."

She nodded. "I thought he'd had an affair with my mother." She shook her head in bewilderment. "But the truth is so much stranger."

"And more dangerous. The long-lost twin of the cherished murdered daughter poses a huge threat. Kevin wants Jack's money and he doesn't like to share."

"But I don't care about the money."

"I believe you, but Kevin won't. Money is everything to him."

Shea frowned. "Kevin must have been the one who broke into your apartment," she said slowly.

"Right. Only he wasn't stealing anything. He was planting evidence."

"Finding Kirsten's ring is what convinced me I couldn't trust you."

"I didn't kill her."

"I know that now. I think I must have known it then, but I was already upset because you'd called me Kirsten and that clouded my judgment."

"Shea, you've got to find a way out of here. Kevin will be back soon to finish us off."

"I thought . . . I thought he'd just leave us here to die." Her eyes looked huge.

Teague started to shake his head, then changed his mind when the pain kicked in. "Too chancy. Someone might find us here, and then, of course, suspicion would fall on him. He's too smart for that. No, I suspect he's out there right now, arranging a fatal 'accident.' It's hard to say how long he'll be gone. Our best hope is for you to go to the sheriff for help. He knows I came out to keep an eye on you. In fact, I'm supposed to check in with the dispatcher once an hour."

"Check in how?"

"On my cell phone."

"Why didn't you say you had a cell phone?"

Teague hated to quench the glimmer of hope in her eyes. " 'Had' is the operative word. Kevin took it."

"But the sheriff knows you're here. When you don't call in, he'll get worried and come looking for you, right?"

Teague shrugged. "Unless the dispatcher's so busy she forgets to mention it to him. No, like I said before, our best bet for survival is for you to go for help."

"How? The trapdoor is nailed shut."

"Yes, but the cellar is really just a hole in the ground. Dirt," he said. "We've got hands. We can dig."

"Dig," she echoed. "I'm an idiot. The spade. That must be why I had to bring it."

"What?"

"I have a spade down here somewhere." She scrambled around on her hands and knees searching for it. "Here it is." She brandished it in triumph.

"Kevin doesn't know you have it?"

"How could he? He followed you, not me." She stood up. "Where should I start digging?"

"Back wall as high up as you can reach."

It was awkward trying to dig a hole at shoulder level, but the ground was surprisingly soft, almost as if it had been disturbed recently. As it had, she remembered. Beelzebub had been buried in the soft wet earth behind the cabin.

"Hurry," Teague said.

"Why? Do you hear him coming?" Shea glanced nervously over her shoulder.

"No, the flashlight batteries are beginning to fail."

She studied the light. Teague was right. It was definitely dimmer. She attacked the hole with renewed energy. Ten minutes later she hit something hard, something that thunked solidly against the spade. Shock waves reverberated down her arms, and she swore under her breath.

"What happened?"

"I hit a rock or something."

"Can you work it loose?"

"I'm trying." She levered the shovel underneath, then along the sides to loosen the big stone. Working carefully so that she didn't start an avalanche, Shea dug around the rock, then inserted the tip of the spade under the obstruction and exerted an upward pressure. The rock popped free like a cork from a bottle, rolling across the cellar to come to rest at Teague's feet.

"Now I'm making some progress," she said with satisfaction.

"Shea?" Teague's voice sounded strange.

She turned to face him. "What?"

"That rock," he said, lifting it gingerly, "isn't a rock. It's a skull."

She recoiled violently. "Left over from the massacre?"

He shook his head slightly. "I don't think so."

"Kirsten?" She shuddered.

He nodded.

"Oh, God. I think I know why Kevin killed the dog. Beelzebub must have disturbed Kirsten's grave. The other day he dropped a bone under Kirsten's bed. It never occurred to me until now that it might have been a human bone."

"So Kevin killed the dog and tossed his body in a shallow grave."

"He must have been in a hurry," she said, eyeing the skull in horrified fascination. "Maybe he was supposed to be running an errand." She remembered the day he'd returned from a trip to the post office with his shoes caked with mud, the same black mud she was now so liberally smeared with.

Shea returned to her digging, praying she wouldn't hit another bony obstruction. She already felt like a grave robber.

Fifteen minutes later the flashlight blinked once,

flickered, then went out. "Batteries just died," Teague announced.

Cold despair squeezed her heart. "The way we will if Kevin has his way."

"Don't give up yet," Teague said. "I may have a minor miracle at my command. There. That should do it." The light returned, much brighter than before.

"How did you do that?"

"Exchanged the old batteries for the ones from my broken flashlight."

"You're a genius." She grinned, despite her fatigue. Her muscles burned and hands were a mess. The gloves had helped, but she knew her palms were blistered and possibly bleeding. Only fear kept her digging.

"Damn," Teague whispered.

"What?" She turned to see a grim expression on his face.

"Kevin's back," he said.

She cocked her head to listen and heard the sound of footsteps crossing the floor above them.

"What do we do now?" She stared at Teague, her mind blank. This wasn't the way it was supposed to end. Dammit, she and Teague had come through so much. They deserved a happily-ever-after.

"Play it by ear," he said calmly. He dragged himself away from the ladder. "Bring me the shovel. I'll play possum, shielding it from view with my body. He doesn't know we have a shovel. And what he doesn't know might hurt him." Teague smiled steadily at her. She knew he was trying to bolster her courage and she loved him for it even though it didn't work.

The nails made a ripping sound as Kevin pulled them from the wood. "He's coming," she said. Right before

Teague doused the light, he winked at her, a frivolous gesture that brought tears of love to her eyes.

Kevin lifted the door and shone his flashlight directly into her face. "Thanks for waiting," he said with a laugh. "Where's your boyfriend? Hiding in the corner to ambush me?"

"Look to your left." Her voice was thick with loathing.

He swung his flashlight across to illuminate Teague's body sprawled lifelessly in the dirt. "Break his back?" he inquired pleasantly.

"He needs a doctor."

"You really don't expect me to rush him to the hospital, do you?"

"Why not? Nobody has to know what really happened. We can claim it was an accident. Like with Daddy and the water hemlock."

"So you figured that out, did you?"

"All except why."

"He was going to change his will. You were going to be added, cutting into my share, and I was going to be stuck with a lousy trust fund. Not acceptable. I need the cash."

"Why? Been gambling again?" she asked. "I thought you'd given up betting on football games."

"Wasn't football this time. Taggart Walsh arranged some private poker games at the club."

Shea frowned. "Taggart Walsh? Isn't he the man who backed into your Fiat?"

"Right. Subtlety's not his strong suit. Trashing my car was a warning. I owe him a bundle." Kevin shrugged. "I've been on a losing streak all summer and Walsh is getting impatient for his money."

"So why not ask Jack?"

"Been there, done that. Decided I don't like the accompanying lectures. Besides, I'm not a beggar."

"No," Shea said. "You're a murderer."

"And a realist. Money's what matters in this world. People are expendable. I learned that lesson early."

"Kirsten," she said. "Why did you kill her, Kevin? You were only twelve. What drove you to murder her?"

"Whatever Kirsten wanted, Kirsten got—a new dress, a new car, a fancy wedding. But whenever I wanted anything, the answer was no."

The trip to the South of France with Jeremy Bancroft's family. Kirsten's thought flashed through her brain. "You wanted to spend the month of August in Saint-Tropez, didn't you? Only Jack said no because if you went, you'd miss Kirsten's wedding."

He gave her a sharp look. "How do you know that?"

"I know a lot of things." She eyed him steadily. "You're the one who broke into Teague's apartment to plant evidence. And you're the one who sent me the anonymous warning."

"Too bad you didn't take it to heart."

"You won't get away with this, Kevin."

He laughed. "Don't be so sure. I'm going to be very rich, and money is power."

His eyes shone bright blue in the glow of his flashlight. Shea wondered how she could ever have mistaken their soulless emptiness for innocence.

"Kirsten ruined everything for me. So I ruined everything for her. Simple as that." Kevin's smile made her shiver.

"My God," she said, swallowing her disgust. "You

killed your sister just because you didn't get to go to the Riviera?"

"Stepsister," he said. "And it wasn't the first time she got in my way." He chuckled. "Though it *was* the last."

"And tonight? Were you the one who tried to smother Daddy?"

Kevin's laughter sounded genuinely amused. "I'm afraid I misled you a bit. There was no attack on Dad tonight. I didn't rush to his bedside. In fact, I never left the island."

"But the calls you made from the hospital . . ." she protested.

"I used the Griffins' phone. Glory let me in. She'd do anything for me."

"I see. Very clever." Obviously his monstrous ego needed some stroking.

He smiled in self-satisfaction. "So now that we understand each other, let's get on with this." Kevin set his big square flashlight at the edge of the opening, then drew a lethal-looking pistol from the waistband of his jeans.

"What are you going to do?" she asked, edging away as he started down the ladder.

"Tie up some loose ends."

"Killing us won't solve anything," Shea said, hoping he'd lose his balance on the missing rung.

He avoided it adroitly, obviously quite familiar with the ladder's idiosyncrasies. "I'm not going to kill anyone. You and lover boy there are going to have an accident."

"What kind of accident?"

"Fatal." He grinned wolfishly, grabbing her sore shoulder.

She winced as much in revulsion as pain. He spun her

around and shoved her roughly against the ladder, slamming her into the rough wood facefirst. Stunned by the unexpected attack, Shea felt the warmth of blood trickling down her forehead.

She turned to face him. "It's no use, Skeeter. You can't kill me. It didn't work the last time, and it won't work this time, either."

"What the hell are you babbling about, Shea McKenzie?" he demanded sharply, but as he stared down at her, a hint of uncertainty clouded his face.

"Not Shea McKenzie. Kirsten Rainey." She shoved the aquamarine crystal cluster under his nose. "Remember this? You should. You're the one who gave it to me. It connects us, Skeeter. Remember the last time you tried to kill me? When you hit me over the head? I had the crystal in my hand then too, didn't I? You startled me when you sneaked up from behind. My hand tightened reflexively, and the rock left diagonal slashes across my fingers, didn't it?"

"How did you know?" His voice was a strangled whisper.

Shea smiled, holding his gaze captive as she placed the crystal cluster on the floor. Slowly she removed the glove and blood-soaked bandages to display her wounds. "Remember?"

Kevin's eyes rolled wildly. "I don't believe it. You can't be Kirsten. Kirsten's dead. I buried her."

"Then how did I know about Saint-Tropez, Skeeter? And the cuts? And the fact that you caved my skull in?"

"I don't believe in ghosts." His voice shook on the last word. Shea sensed rather than saw the movement behind him.

"Do you believe in possession?"

"I'll show you possession." Kevin jammed the barrel of the pistol against the base of her throat.

Had she pushed him too far in her efforts to distract him? She tasted the sour flavor of fear but forced herself to speak coolly. "You can keep destroying the bodies, but not the spirit. I'll come back again and again until you pay for what you did." Her words ended in a gasp as Kevin ground the gun barrel into the vulnerable flesh of her exposed throat.

Teague sat up, slamming the spade into the backs of Kevin's knees. Kevin's mouth formed an O of surprise and he buckled like a broken toy. Shea dove sideways into the darkness, scrambling in the dirt for a weapon. She knew the broken flashlight lay somewhere nearby. But the object her searching fingers located wasn't a flashlight. It was bigger and lighter. Kirsten's poor damaged skull, she realized.

Strangely, as she held the skull in her bloodied hands, her desperate fear began to ease. Warmth and power seemed to flow into her weary body like an electric current. Across the width of the cellar, the crystal glowed with an unearthly radiance.

Kevin regained his balance, but not before Teague got in another good shot with the spade. Furious, Kevin aimed a savage kick at the side of Teague's head. The older man was able to avoid the brunt of the blow, but he absorbed enough of the impact to send him sprawling. Recovering himself, Kevin leveled his pistol at Teague's chest.

"No!" Shea screamed, diverting Kevin's attention for a split second.

Teague, breathing hard, his teeth bared in an expression like that of a cornered animal's, scrabbled sideways, then swung the spade back for one final blow.

Kevin saw none of this. All his concentration was trained on Shea. He glared at her, his face a vicious mask of hatred. "Okay, fine. Ladies first."

Shea watched numbly as the pistol swung in her direction. She squeezed the skull between her hands. *Kirsten, help me!*

Gladly, sister. I've been waiting seven years for this moment. The words washed through Shea's head on a wave of cold fury.

Then everything seemed to switch to slow motion. One minute Kevin was glowering down the sights at her, and the next his face seemed to crumple in upon itself in an expression of terror. "Kirsten?" His voice rose two octaves in as many syllables.

"Kirsten?" echoed Teague, his hand going momentarily slack on the spade handle.

A low humming throbbed in Shea's ears, drowning out all other sound. A strange, bluish light bathed the cellar.

"Give it up. You can't kill me." Kirsten held the skull aloft. "Exhibit A, Skeeter. I'm already dead, remember?"

Kevin's face blanched. A muscle twitched in his jaw. "You may be dead, but Harris isn't. Yet." He turned the gun on Teague.

Kirsten's pent-up fury exploded. With a blood-curdling yell, she split away from Shea, flinging herself and the skull at Kevin's face.

❦⎯⎯❦

Shea dove for the gun, which flew off into the shadows as Kevin fought to protect himself, clawing madly at the skull.

Her hands closed over the reassuringly solid grip of the pistol, and she turned to see what was happening.

"Freeze," she ordered, unnecessarily as it turned out. Kevin was crumpled against the ladder, his face a frozen mask of horror. The damaged skull rested on his chest. Teague lay slumped nearby. Both men looked dead.

"Teague?" she whispered.

Up above, Kevin's flashlight wobbled as heavy footsteps shook the floor of the cabin. "Harris? Are you all right? Harris? Can you hear me?"

Teague moved then and she saw his expression. He looked as if he'd seen a ghost. And maybe he had. "Down here, Sheriff," he called.

EPILOGUE

Shea perched on an ugly and wretchedly uncomfortable chair beside Teague's bed, waiting for him to open his eyes. She'd been there so long, she'd memorized the fire escape plan taped to the inside of the door and counted all the holes in the acoustic tile ceiling. Two thousand seven hundred and ninety-five in case anyone was interested.

"Come on, Teague. Open your eyes already."

Not a flutter.

She sighed in resignation. He'd been out of the recovery room for almost forty minutes now. The nurse said he was just sleeping off the residual effects of the anesthetic. Nothing to worry about. But Shea went ahead and worried, anyway. What if Teague's head injury was more serious than they thought? What if he was in a coma, not sleeping at all? What if he suddenly stopped breathing altogether?

He groaned in his sleep and burrowed his head into the flat hospital pillow. So okay, he wasn't dead, and maybe the medical professionals knew what they were talking about. Maybe.

Jack had flown in a team of hotshot orthopedic surgeons from Boise to patch Teague's shattered legs back together with steel pins. The healing process would be slow and painful, and his right knee was going to require further surgery. But at least he was alive.

As was Kevin. In a manner of speaking.

Kevin. She shuddered. How could anyone be so blinded by greed? If he'd managed to eliminate her and Teague, who'd have been next on his hit list? His mother? Mikey?

Teague's eyes flickered open. "My legs?" he asked in a surprisingly strong voice.

She smiled reassurance. "Good as new or they soon will be."

He shut his eyes for a second, then opened them again, suddenly alert. "And Kevin?"

"In Missoula for psychiatric evaluation, though I doubt they'll learn much. He's catatonic."

Teague grunted. "It's a wonder I'm not. That was quite a show you and Kirsten put on. What did you tell Sheriff Carlton?"

"The truth. Or as much of it as I thought he'd believe—that Kevin freaked out when I tossed the skull at him."

Teague nodded. "I was there. I saw what happened, and I'm still not sure *I* believe it." He grinned. "Maybe they ought to ship me off to Missoula to have my head examined." He fell silent for a moment, then asked, "How're Jack and Cynthia holding up?"

"Better than I would under the circumstances. Jack was understandably surprised to discover he had another daughter. But pleased, I think. Cynthia's pretty upset about Kevin's part in all of this, but she's hanging in there for Mikey's sake."

"Jack's handling Kirsten's death all right?"

"As well as could be expected." Shea swallowed hard. "He's arranged to have her remains moved to the family plot."

Teague stared at the ceiling, silent for so long that Shea started to worry.

"I talked to my mother this morning," she said. "She'd called my godmother, found out where I was."

"And?"

"She confirmed everything Sheriff Carlton said." Shea dug the postcard from her purse and handed it to Teague. "This is what brought me to Liberty in the first place."

Teague read the card. "Jack and Elizabeth didn't know about you, did they?"

"Mom never told them. She was afraid of losing me. She still is, I think."

Teague's expression was remote. "When are you leaving?"

"Leaving?"

"For Ohio." He wouldn't even look at her.

"Since I'm between jobs at the moment, I thought I'd stick around. Permanently, if you'd like." She kept her tone deliberately light.

"What about your mother?"

"She'll come around eventually." She smiled.

He didn't smile back.

Don't upset him, the doctors had warned, but they hadn't said a word about him upsetting her, and dammit, he had that Shea-I'm-sorry look on his face.

"Shea, I'm sorry," he said. "I don't think things are going to work out between us."

She examined her lacerated palm in silence. Already the cuts were beginning to heal. The damage to her heart would take a lot longer to mend.

Her first instinct was to run, to hightail it back to Ohio, where she could hole up and lick her wounds in private, the way she'd done when she'd lost her job. But that was the old Shea's solution. Not hers.

She squared her shoulders. "Why not?" she demanded. "Because you don't love me? Baloney! Because I'm Kirsten's twin? So what? Because I have more money in the bank than you do? Who cares? Because you're temporarily on the injured list? Big deal. I'd love you even if you didn't have legs."

Teague glanced up at her, hot color staining his cheekbones. "Did you just say you loved me?"

"What? Are you deaf? Of course I love you." She grabbed his hand and squeezed. Hard.

"Even after I practically got you killed?"

She raised an eyebrow. "I'm not sure who almost got whom killed. You appear to be in worse shape than I am." She slid off her chair and, still clinging to his hand, dropped to her knees beside the bed.

He frowned. "What are you doing?"

"Your job." She grinned. "Since going down on bended knee is not an option for you at the moment, I'm taking the initiative. My darling, sweet idiot, Teague, will you marry me?"

The harsh planes of his face quivered. "Marry you? Shea, are you sure that's what you want?"

She stood up slowly. Still cradling his big hand between her two smaller ones, she remembered the way his eyes changed right before he kissed her, the way she felt inside when he smiled one of his all-too-rare smiles, the way he'd fought to protect her from Kevin. Oh, yes. She was sure. "Positive," she said.

His eyes turned smoky. A smile tilted the corners of his mouth.

"Is that a yes?" she asked.

"No," he said, "but this is." And pulling her close, he kissed her pretty much nonstop until the nurse threw her out.

Some things were worth fighting for.

THE EDITORS' CORNER

The heat is on and nowhere is that more evident than right here at Loveswept. This month's selections include some of our most romantic titles yet. Take one mechanic, one television talk-show host, a masseuse, and a travel agent, then combine them with strong, to-die-for heroes, and you've got yourself one heck of a month's worth of love stories.

Loveswept favorite Mary Kay McComas returns with **ONE ON ONE**, LOVESWEPT #894. Mechanic Michelin Albee has no idea what she's getting into when she picks up stranded motorist Noah Tessler on a lonely stretch of desert highway. Noah's purpose in coming to Gypsum, Nevada, is to meet the woman who captured his late brother's heart and gave birth to Eric, Noah's only living relative. Uncharacteristically, Mich takes a liking to Noah. Trusting him more than she's trusted any man in the past few years, she confides in him about her worries for Eric. As

Noah gets closer to both Mich and her son, will he be able to keep his secret? Once again Mary Kay McComas grabs our hearts in a book as deliciously romantic as a bouquet of wildflowers in a teacup!

In Kathy Lynn Emerson's latest contribution, we learn that love is best when it's **TRIED AND TRUE**, LOVESWEPT #895. Because Vanessa Dare has more than a passing interest in history, she agrees to produce a documentary about professor Grant Bradley's living history center in western New York. Grant knows that having the television talk-show host on the project will bring him the exposure Westbrook Farm needs, but he's surprised when desire sizzles between them. When Nessa doesn't balk at sacrificing present-day comforts, Grant realizes he just might have found the perfect woman. She's content merely to get away from the pressures of work, and as they play the part of an 1890s courting couple, the sweet hunger that transpires could prove to be their destiny. As riveting as the pages of a secret diary, Kathy Lynn Emerson's delectable story of love's mysteries and history's magic is utterly charming.

Donna Kauffman is at her best when she gives us a witty romp, and **TEASE ME**, LOVESWEPT #896, is nothing less. Tucker Morgan knows that his life needs a change. He's just not so sure that posing as a masseur is a change for the better. But since he promised his aunt Lillian he'd investigate the shady goings-on at her Florida retirement community, he'd better take a serious look at those instructional videos she gave him. Sent in to evaluate the new masseur's skills, Lainey Cooper knew she was in trouble from the moment he touched her. If his magical hands turned her knees to mush, Lord knew what he could do to the rest of her body! Aunt Lillian is sure something's happening at Sunset Shores, and insists Lainey and

Tucker team up to uncover its secrets . . . and if a little romance is thrown in on the side, hey, what more can an elderly aunt ask for her nephew? Donna Kauffman delivers a sparkling tale of equal parts mystery and matchmaking.

Welcome Suzanne McMinn, who makes her Loveswept debut with **UNDENIABLE,** LOVE-SWEPT #897. After his wife left him stranded with four daughters to raise, Garth Holloway decided he wasn't going to add any more women to his life. And when his pretty neighbor Kelly Thompson popped out of a Halloween casket, scaring his youngest child nearly to death, he knew his decision was right. Kelly isn't going to argue with him. She's through with raising children. With her younger siblings now in college, she's free to go wherever her heart desires. But when an undeniable passion reigns, Garth and Kelly can't stay away from each other. His children adore her, not to mention the family dog. Garth doesn't want to hold her back, but faced with unconditional love, will Kelly grab her passport or surrender her solo ticket for a hunk on the family plan? Suzanne McMinn's tale of dreams deferred and temptations tasted is as heartwarming as it is irresistible.

Happy reading!

With warmest wishes,

Susann Brailey *Joy Abella*

Susann Brailey   Joy Abella
Senior Editor   Administrative Editor

P.S. Look for these women's fiction titles coming in July! Deborah Smith returns with **WHEN VENUS FELL.** A novel of two sisters, seeking refuge from their troubled past, who find love and acceptance amid the shattered remains of a tight-knit family in the mountains of Tennessee. From nationally bestselling author Kay Hooper comes **FINDING LAURA,** now available in paperback. A collector of mirrors, struggling artist Laura Sutherland stumbles across an antique hand mirror that lands her in the midst of the powerful Kilbourne family and a legacy of deadly intent. And fun and laughter abound in **FINDING MR. RIGHT** by Bantam newcomer Emily Carmichael. A femme fatale must return to Earth to find the right man for her best friend. The trouble is, when you're a Welsh corgi, there's only so much you can do to play matchmaker! And immediately following this page, preview the Bantam women's fiction titles on sale in July.

For current information on Bantam's women's fiction, visit our website at the following address:
http://www.bdd.com/romance

Don't miss these exciting
novels from Bantam Books!

On sale in June:

GENUINE LIES
by Nora Roberts

THE HOSTAGE
BRIDE
by Jane Feather

THE WEDDING
CHASE
by Rebecca Kelley

Genuine Lies
BY NORA ROBERTS

She was a legend. A product of time and talent and her own unrelenting ambition. Eve Benedict. Men thirty years her junior desired her. Women envied her. Studio heads courted her, knowing that in this day when movies were made by accountants, her name was solid gold. In a career that had spanned nearly fifty years, Eve Benedict had known the highs, and the lows, and used both to forge herself into what she wanted to be.

She did as she chose, personally and professionally. If a role interested her, she went after it with the same verve and ferocity she'd used to get her first part. If she desired a man, she snared him, discarding him only when she was done, and—she liked to brag—never with malice. All of her former lovers, and they were legion, remained friends. Or had the good sense to pretend to be.

At sixty-seven, Eve had maintained her magnificent body through discipline and the surgeon's art. Over a half century she had honed herself into a sharp blade. She had used both disappointment and triumph to temper that blade into a weapon that was feared and respected in the kingdom of Hollywood.

She had been a goddess. Now she was a queen with a keen mind and keen tongue. Few knew her heart. None knew her secrets.

❖————❖

Julia wasn't certain if she'd just been given the world's most fascinating Christmas present or an enormous lump of coal. She stood at the big bay window of her Connecticut home and watched the wind hurl the snow in a blinding white dance. Across the room, the logs snapped and sizzled in the wide stone fireplace. A bright red stocking hung on either end of the mantel. Idly, she spun a silver star and sent it twirling on its bough of the blue spruce.

The tree was square in the center of the window, precisely where Brandon had wanted it. They had chosen the six-foot spruce together, had hauled it, puffing and blowing, into the living room, then had spent an entire evening decorating. Brandon had known where he'd wanted every ornament. When she would have tossed the tinsel at the branches in hunks, he had insisted on draping individual strands.

He'd already chosen the spot where they would plant it on New Year's Day, starting a new tradition in their new home in a new year.

At ten, Brandon was a fiend for tradition. Perhaps, she thought, because he had never known a traditional home. Thinking of her son, Julia looked down at the presents stacked under the tree. There, too, was order. Brandon had a ten-year-old's need to shake and sniff and rattle the brightly wrapped boxes. He had the curiosity, and the wit, to cull out hints on what was hidden inside. But when he replaced a box, it went neatly into its space.

In a few hours he would begin to beg his mother to let him open one—just one—present tonight, on Christmas Eve. That, too, was tradition. She would refuse. He would cajole. She would pretend reluctance. He would persuade. And this year, she thought, at last, they would celebrate their Christmas in a real home. Not in an apartment in downtown Manhattan, but a house, a home, with a yard made for snowmen, a big kitchen designed for baking cookies. She'd so badly needed to be able to give him all this. She hoped it helped to make up for not being able to give him a father.

Turning from the window, she began to wander around the room. A small, delicate-looking woman in an oversized flannel shirt and baggy jeans, she always dressed comfortably in private to rest from being the scrupulously groomed, coolly professional public woman. Julia Summers prided herself on the image she presented to publishers, television audiences, the celebrities she interviewed. She was pleased by her skill in interviews, finding out what she needed to know about others while they learned very little about her.

Her press kit informed anyone who wanted to know that she had grown up in Philadelphia, an only child of two successful lawyers. It granted the information that she had attended Brown University, and that she was a single parent. It listed her professional accomplishments, her awards. But it didn't speak of the hell she had lived through in the three years before her parents had divorced, or the fact that she had brought her son into the world alone at age eighteen. There was no mention of the grief she had felt when she had lost her mother, then her father within two years of each other in her mid-twenties.

Though she had never made a secret of it, it was far from common knowledge that she had been adopted when she was six weeks old, and that nearly eighteen years to the day after had given birth to a baby boy whose father was listed on the birth certificate as unknown.

Julia didn't consider the omissions lies—though, of course, she had known the name of Brandon's father. The simple fact was, she was too smooth an interviewer to be trapped into revealing anything she didn't wish to reveal.

And, amused by being able so often to crack façades, she enjoyed being the public Ms. Summers who wore her dark blond hair in a sleek French twist, who chose trim, elegant suits in jewel tones, who could appear on *Donahue* or *Carson* or *Oprah* to tout a new book without showing a trace of the hot, sick nerves that lived inside the public package.

When she came home, she wanted only to be Julia. Brandon's mother. A woman who liked cooking her son's dinner, dusting furniture, planning a garden. Making a home was her most vital work and writing made it possible.

Now, as she waited for her son to come bursting in the door to tell her all about sledding with the neighbors, she thought of the offer her agent had just called her about. It had come out of the blue.

Eve Benedict.

Still pacing restlessly, Julia picked up and replaced knickknacks, plumped pillows on the sofa, rearranged magazines. The living room was a lived-in mess that was more her doing than Brandon's. As she fiddled with the position of a vase of dried flowers or the angle of a china dish, she stepped over kicked-off shoes, ignored a basket of laundry yet to be folded. And considered.

Eve Benedict. The name ran through her head like magic. This was not merely a celebrity, but a woman who had earned the right to be called star. Her talent and her temperament were as well known and as well respected as her face. A face, Julia thought, that had graced movie screens for almost fifty years, in over a hundred films. Two Oscars, a Tony, four husbands—those were only a few of the awards that lined her trophy case. She had known the Hollywood of Bogart and Gable; she had survived, even triumphed, in the days when the studio system gave way to the accountants.

After nearly fifty years in the spotlight, this would be Benedict's first authorized biography. Certainly it was the first time the star had contacted an author and offered her complete cooperation. With strings, Julia reminded herself, and sunk onto the couch. It was those strings that had forced her to tell her agent to stall.

She thrilled with her "V" series. She dazzled with her "Charm Bracelet" trilogy. Now, following nine consecutive national bestsellers, Jane Feather takes on readers' favorite topic with the first novel in an enthralling "bride" trilogy.

The Hostage Bride
BY JANE FEATHER

Bride #1 is the outspoken Portia. . . . It's bad enough that seventeen-year-old Portia Worth is taken in by her uncle, the marquis of Granville, after her father dies. As the bastard niece, Portia knows she can expect little beyond a roof over her head and a place at the table. But it truly adds insult to injury when the Granville's archenemy, the outlaw Rufus Decatur, hatches a scheme to abduct the marquis's daughter—only to kidnap Portia by accident. Portia, who possesses more than a streak of independence as well as a talent for resistance, does not take kindly to being abducted—mistakenly or otherwise. Decatur will soon find himself facing the challenge of his life, both on the battle-field and in the bedroom, as he contends with this misfit of a girl who has the audacity to believe herself the equal of any man. . . .

"Now just who do we have here?"

Portia drew the reins tight. The quivering horse raised its head and neighed in protest, pawing the ground. Portia looked up and into a pair of vivid blue eyes glinting with an amusement to match the voice.

"And who are you?" she demanded. "And why have you taken those men prisoner?"

Her hood had fallen back in her struggles with the horse and Rufus found himself the object of a fierce green-eyed scrutiny from beneath an unruly tangle of hair as orange-red as a burning brazier. Her complexion was white as milk, but not from fear, he decided; she looked far too annoyed for alarm.

"Rufus Decatur, Lord Rothbury, at your service," he said solemnly, removing his plumed hat with a flourish as he offered a mock bow from atop his great chestnut stallion. "And who is it who travels under the Granville standard? If you please . . ." He raised a bushy red eyebrow.

Portia didn't answer the question. "Are you abducting us? Or is it murder you have in mind?"

"Tell you what," Rufus said amiably, catching her mount's bridle just below the bit. "We'll trade questions. But let's continue this fascinating but so far uninformative exchange somewhere a little less exposed to this ball-breaking cold."

Portia reacted without thought. Her whip hand rose and she slashed at Decatur's wrist, using all her force so that the blow cut through the leather gauntlet. He gave a shout of surprise, his hand falling from the bridle, and Portia had gathered the reins, kicked at the animal's flanks, and was racing down the track, neither knowing nor caring in which direction, before Rufus fully realized what had happened.

Portia heard him behind her, the chestnut's pounding hooves cracking the thin ice that had formed over the wet mud between the ridges on the track. She urged her horse to greater speed and the animal, still panicked from the earlier melee, threw up his head and plunged forward. If she had given him his head he would have bolted but she hung on, maintaining some semblance of control, crouched low over his neck, half expecting a musket shot from behind.

But she knew this was a race she wasn't going to win. Her horse was a neat, sprightly young gelding, but he hadn't the stride or the deep chest of the pursuing animal. Unless Rufus Decatur decided for some reason to give up the chase, she was going to be overtaken within minutes. And then she realized that her pursuer was not overtaking her, he was keeping an even distance between them, and for some reason this infuriated Portia. It was as if he was playing with her, cat with mouse, allowing her to think she was escaping even as he waited to pounce in his own good time.

She slipped her hand into her boot, her fingers closing over the hilt of the wickedly sharp dagger Jack had insisted she carry from the moment he had judged her mature enough to attract unwelcome attention. By degrees, she drew back on the reins, slowing the horse's mad progress even as she straightened in the saddle. The hooves behind her were closer now. She waited, wanting him to be too close to stop easily. Her mind was cold and clear, her heart steady, her breathing easy. But she was ready to do murder.

With a swift jerk, she pulled up her horse, swinging round in the saddle in the same moment, the dagger in her hand, the weight of the hilt balanced between her index and forefingers, steadied by her thumb.

Rufus Decatur was good and close and as she'd hoped his horse was going fast enough to carry him right past her before he could pull it up. She saw his startled expression as for a minute he was facing her head on. She threw the dagger, straight for his heart.

It lodged in his chest, piercing his thick cloak.

The hilt quivered. Portia, mesmerized, stared at it, for the moment unable to kick her horse into motion again. She had never killed a man before.

"Jesus, Mary, and sainted Joseph!" Rufus Decatur exclaimed in a voice far too vigorous for that of a dead man. He pulled the dagger free and looked down at it in astonishment. "Mother of God!" He regarded the girl on her horse in astonishment. "You were trying to stab me!"

Portia was as astonished as he was, but for rather different reasons. She could see no blood on the blade. And then the mystery was explained. Her intended victim moved aside his cloak to reveal a thickly padded buff coat of the kind soldiers wore. It was fair protection against knives and arrows, if not musket balls.

"You were chasing me," she said, feeling no need to apologize for her murderous intent. Indeed, she sounded as cross as she felt. "You abducted my escort and you were chasing me. Of course I wanted to stop you."

Rufus thought that most young women finding themselves in such a situation, if they hadn't swooned away in fright or thrown a fit of strong hysterics first, would have chosen a less violent course of action. But this tousled and indignant member of the female sex obviously had a rather more down to earth attitude, one with which he couldn't help but find himself in sympathy.

"Well, I suppose you have a point," he agreed, turning the knife over in his hand. His eyes were speculative as he examined the weapon. It was no toy. He looked up, subjecting her to a sharp scrutiny. "I should have guessed that a lass with that hair would have a temper to match."

"As it happens, I don't," Portia said, returning his scrutiny with her own, every bit as sharp and a lot less benign. "I'm a very calm and easy-going person in general. Except when someone's chasing me with obviously malicious intent."

"Well, I have to confess I do have the temper to match," Rufus declared with a sudden laugh as he swept off his hat to reveal his own brightly burnished locks. "But it's utterly dormant at present. All I need from you are the answers to a couple of questions, and then you may be on your way again. I simply want to know who you are and why you're riding under Granville protection."

"And what business is it of yours?" Portia demanded.

"Well . . . you see, anything to do with the Granvilles is my business," Rufus explained almost apologetically. "So, I really do need to have the answers to my questions."

"What are you doing with Sergeant Crampton and his men?"

"Oh, just a little sport," he said with a careless flourish of his hat. "They'll come to no real harm, although they might get a little chilly."

Portia looked over her shoulder down the narrow lane. She could see no sign of either the sergeant and his men or Rufus Decatur's men. "Why didn't you overtake me?" She turned back to him, her eyes narrowed. "You could have done so any time you chose."

"You were going in the right direction so I saw no need," he explained reasonably. "Shall we continue on our way?"

The right direction for what?

In the tradition of *New York Times* bestseller Betina Krahn comes a sparkling new talent with a witty, passionate tale of a spinster wary of desire—and the charming rogue who's determined to change her tune. . . .

The Wedding Chase
BY REBECCA KELLEY

Wolfgang Hardwicke, the Earl of Northcliffe, is up to no good—as usual. So he isn't certain why he rescues the drunken gambler from a fight. And he never expects to be rewarded with a heavenly, all-too-brief glimpse of the gambler's exquisite sister, clad only in her nightgown. Nor does he guess that he'll see her again, lighting up a dull party as she plays piano with an unguardedly rapturous expression—an expression Wolfgang would like to see in decidedly different circumstances. . . . Unlike her admirer, Miss Grizelda Fleetwood is an unabashed do-gooder, one who has as soft a heart for her ne'er-do-well brother as for the unfortunates she helps. Though Zel has no interest in matrimony, she's determined to marry to save her family from financial ruin. That is, if she can find a suitable match before the unprincipled and relentless Earl of Northcliffe ruins her reputation . . . or steals her defenseless heart.

Eventually, Wolfgang found himself in the music room. He hadn't practiced in months but, inspired by Miss Fleetwood's performance, he couldn't resist trying his hand. First the pianoforte, then its player.

A smile brushed his lips. Her sweet blush contrasted so intriguingly with her bold behavior. She followed along with his game of cat and mouse, allowing him to sit far too close, moving away only a bit to encourage rather than discourage him. Yet when faced with competition, she deserted the field, leaving him in Isadora's clutches despite his silent plea for aid.

He sighed, seating himself on the bench. If he wished to be an honorable gentleman, any doubts dictated that he leave her alone. But why should he allow a few scruples to interfere with his amusements? And she did amuse him.

He would proceed with flirtation, moving ever so skillfully into seduction. Smiling, Wolfgang rifled through the sheet music arrayed on the pianoforte. Finding a familiar Mozart sonata, he began to softly finger the hardwood keys.

He was thoroughly destroying the piece when he sensed another presence in the room. A spicy scent. Wolfgang turned to see Grizelda Fleetwood, in another dowdy gown, hesitating at the door. He stopped abruptly, surprised at his embarrassment.

"Discovered! The foul deed uncovered!" He smiled, eased the bench back and stood with a flourish. "I confess my guilt. I've murdered Mozart."

She laughed, a throaty sound of full, easy humor that struck a chord within him. Her laughter bore no resemblance to the rehearsed titter affected by the ladies of the *ton*. "I wouldn't call it murder, my lord, maybe a little unintentional mayhem. You have a fine hand, but it's clear you rarely practice."

"The truth is indeed revealed. I seldom, almost never practice. Lacking discipline, I have become a much better listener than player." Wolfgang took a step closer, drawing her eyes to his. "You are quite beyond my touch."

That faint blush appeared again, as she set a well-worn portfolio on the table. "Do you sight read?"

"About as well as I play."

"That will be fine. I have a few Bach pieces my music master arranged for four hands on the pianoforte." Her low voice softened. "The easier part was for my brother. My part acts as the counterpoint. Would you like to try?"

"I would be honored to take instruction." He bowed, sat back on the bench and patted the seat beside him. "But please be kind to your humble pupil, Madam Music Master."

An answering smile lit her face as she opened her portfolio. She pulled out some tattered papers before sitting a respectable distance from him on the bench. He took the music, scanned it quickly and laid it out where they both could see.

Miss Fleetwood removed her eyeglasses, pushed back a wisp of dark brown hair and ran bare fingers lightly over the keys. "Are you ready? My part joins in after the first few measures."

Wolfgang began to tentatively tap out the notes. The piece was easy and his confidence rapidly increased. Soon she joined in, the notes prancing, circling, interlacing playfully. They both reached to turn the page, his hand met hers, skin to skin. A thrumming—a contralto's lowest note—reverberated through him. Their gazes crossed and locked. Suddenly he wanted to touch much more than her fingers. As if he'd spoken the thought aloud, she looked away, stumbling over the next measure. She seemed to draw herself in, her slender form compact and contained, and continued the piece. He inhaled slowly, breathing in her scent, and found his place in the music, barely missing a note.

As they finished the arrangement, she turned to him with what might have been a smile had her mouth not been so tight. "I believe you could be quite good if you applied yourself."

The corner of his lips twitched as he restrained an answering smile. "I'm always good when I apply myself, Miss Fleetwood." The threatening grin broke through. "But speaking of good, you should see me ride. Do you ride?"

"Ride? What do you . . ." She hesitated slightly. "I ride, but not well."

"Good. I've played your student, now you'll play mine."

On sale in July:

WHEN VENUS FELL
by Deborah Smith

FINDING LAURA
by Kay Hooper

*FINDING
MR. RIGHT*
by Emily Carmichael

Bestselling Historical Women's Fiction

⊱ IRIS JOHANSEN ⊰

⊱ TERESA MEDEIROS ⊰

Ask for these books at your local bookstore or use this page to order.

Please send me the books I have checked above. I am enclosing $____ (add $2.50 to cover postage and handling). Send check or money order, no cash or C.O.D.'s, please.

Name _____

Address _____

City/State/Zip _____

Send order to: Bantam Books, Dept. FN 16, 2451 S. Wolf Rd., Des Plaines, IL 60018

Allow four to six weeks for delivery.

Prices and availability subject to change without notice.   FN 16 6/98

Bestselling Historical Women's Fiction

✳AMANDA QUICK✳

_____28354-5 SEDUCTION . . .$6.50/$8.99 Canada

_____28932-2 SCANDAL . . . .$6.50/$8.99

_____28594-7 SURRENDER . . . .$6.50/$8.99

_____29325-7 RENDEZVOUS . . . .$6.50/$8.99

_____29315-X RECKLESS . . . .$6.50/$8.99

_____29316-8 RAVISHED . . . .$6.50/$8.99

_____29317-6 DANGEROUS . . . .$6.50/$8.99

_____56506-0 DECEPTION . . . .$6.50/$8.99

_____56153-7 DESIRE . . . .$6.50/$8.99

_____56940-6 MISTRESS . . . .$6.50/$8.99

_____57159-1 MYSTIQUE . . . .$6.50/$7.99

_____57190-7 MISCHIEF . . . .$6.50/$8.99

_____57407-8 AFFAIR . . . .$6.99/$8.99

✳IRIS JOHANSEN✳

_____29871-2 LAST BRIDGE HOME . . .$5.50/$7.50

_____29604-3 THE GOLDEN

BARBARIAN . . . .$6.99/$8.99

_____29244-7 REAP THE WIND . . . . . .$5.99/$7.50

_____29032-0 STORM WINDS . . . .$6.99/$8.99

Ask for these books at your local bookstore or use this page to order.

Please send me the books I have checked above. I am enclosing $_____ (add $2.50 to cover postage and handling). Send check or money order, no cash or C.O.D.'s, please.

Name _____

Address _____

City/State/Zip _____

Send order to: Bantam Books, Dept. FN 16, 2451 S. Wolf Rd., Des Plaines, IL 60018
Allow four to six weeks for delivery.
Prices and availability subject to change without notice.   FN 16 6/98